Brenda Jackson is a *New York Times* bestselling author of more than one hundred romance titles. Brenda lives in Jacksonville, Florida, and divides her time between family, writing and travelling.

Email Brenda at authorbrendajackson@gmail.com or visit her on her website at brendajackson.net.

An Honourable Seduction

BRENDA JACKSON

MILLS & BOON

First published in Great Britain 2018
by Mills & Boon, an imprint of HarperCollins*Publishers*
1 London Bridge Street, London, SE1 9GF

Large Print edition 2018

© 2018 Brenda Streater Jackson

ISBN: 978-0-263-07787-2

MIX
Paper from
responsible sources
FSC™ C007454

This book is produced from independently certified
FSC™ paper to ensure responsible forest management.
For more information visit www.harpercollins.co.uk/green.

Printed and bound in Great Britain
by CPI Group (UK) Ltd, Croydon, CR0 4YY

To the man who will forever be the love of my life, Gerald Jackson, Sr.

To all of my readers who asked for Flipper's story. This one is for you!

To the Brenda Jackson Book Club/ Facebook fans. Over 4,000 strong and after fourteen years, you guys still rock!

Many waters cannot quench love; rivers cannot sweep it away.
                              —*Song of Solomon* 8:7

Prologue

"What kind of trouble have you gotten into?"

David Holloway, known to his Navy SEAL teammates as Flipper, glanced at the four men surrounding him. They were like brothers to him. More than once they'd risked their lives for each other and they would continue to have each other's backs, on duty or off. That bond was what accounted for the concerned looks on their faces.

He wondered how they'd known he'd been summoned to the admiral's office.

"Let's hope I'm not in any trouble, Mac," Flipper said, rubbing a hand down his face.

He had to admit he was wondering what was going on, just like they were. Usually, you were only summoned to a meeting with the admiral when you were getting reprimanded for some reason, and he never got into trouble. At least he *rarely* did. As the son of a retired SEALs commanding officer and the youngest of five brothers—all Navy SEALs—he knew better.

"Maybe there's an event on the base and he wants you to escort his daughter now that you're the single one among us," Coop said, grinning.

Flipper didn't grin back. They'd seen Georgianna Martin, the admiral's twenty-three-year-old daughter. She was beautiful, but they'd heard the horror stories from other teammates who'd been ordered to take her out on dates. According to them, those evenings had been the dates from hell. The young woman was spoiled rotten, selfish as sin and had an attitude that sucked. That's why Flipper didn't find Coop's comment at all amusing. He hoped that wasn't why the admiral wanted to see him.

It didn't surprise Flipper that it was Mac who'd asked if Flipper had gotten into trouble. Thurston McRoy—code name Mac—was older than the other four men on the team, who had all started their careers as SEALs around the same time. Mac had been a SEAL five years before the rest of them. Mac seemed to like to think he was the big brother looking out for them, almost like he figured they couldn't take care of themselves. He was forever giving them advice—even when they didn't ask for it.

In addition to Mac and Flipper, their SEAL team included Brisbane Westmoreland, code name Bane; Gavin Blake, whose code name was Viper; and Laramie Cooper, whose code name was Coop.

Flipper checked his watch. "Since I have a couple of hours to spare before meeting with the admiral, let's grab something to eat," he suggested.

"Sounds good to me," Bane said.

Less than an hour later, Flipper and his four teammates shared burgers, fries and milkshakes at one of the most popular eating places on base. They decided to sit outside at one of the café tables in the front instead of inside where it was crowded since it was such a beautiful May day.

No one brought up his meeting with the admiral again or the notion of him taking the admiral's daughter on a date. He was glad. Instead, the guys had more important things to talk about, namely their families.

Bane's wife, Crystal, had given birth to triplets last year and he had new photos to share, so they passed Bane's cell phone around.

Viper's wife, Layla, was expecting with only a few months to go before Gavin Blake IV would be born. Viper was excited about becoming a father, of course.

Like Bane, Mac had plenty of photos to share; he was married and the father of four.

And Coop had a two-year-old son he hadn't known about until he'd run into his old girlfriend about six months ago. They'd reconnected, gotten married and were now a happy family.

Earlier in the week, the teammates had gotten word from their commanding officer that next week was the start of a four-month leave. For Flipper, that meant heading home to Dallas and he couldn't wait. His mother had a birthday coming up and he was glad he would be home to celebrate.

"I don't care what plans you all are making for your leave, just as long as you remember my mom's birthday celebration. I understand you not showing up, Viper, with a baby on the way. The rest of you guys, no excuses."

"We hear you," Bane said, grinning. "And we will be there."

When Viper ordered another hamburger, everyone teased him about being the one to eat for two instead of his wife. And then everyone talked about what they planned to do with their four months off.

It was two hours later when Flipper walked into the admiral's office. He was surprised to find Commanding Officer Shields there as well. Flipper saluted both men.

"At ease. Please have a seat, Lieutenant Holloway."

"Thank you, sir," he said, sitting down. He was used to being under his commanding officer's intense scrutiny, but there was something in the sharp green eyes of Admiral Norris Martin that was making him feel uncomfortable.

"You come highly recommended by your commanding officer here, Lieutenant Holloway. And the reason I asked to meet with you is that we need you. Your country needs you."

Flipper was happy to step up. He was a Navy SEAL, and the reason he'd enlisted, like his father and brothers, was to protect his country. "And what am I needed to do, sir?" he asked.

"Our investigators have provided intelligence and a preliminary report that says acts of espionage are happening in Key West. Someone is trading valuable government secrets to China."

Flipper didn't respond immediately.

The one thing he hated was a traitor, but he'd

discovered that for the right price, a number of American citizens would perform acts of treason. He understood that. However, what he didn't understand was why he'd been singled out for this meeting. He was part of a SEAL team. He didn't work in naval intelligence.

Confusion must have shown on his face because Admiral Martin continued, "The report was given to me, but I don't believe it."

Flipper raised a brow. "You don't believe a report that classified documents are being traded in Key West, sir?"

"Oh, I believe all that, but what I refuse to believe is that this suspect is guilty of anything."

"Is there a reason why, sir?"

"Here is the information," said Commanding Officer Shields, speaking for the first time as he handed Flipper a folder.

Flipper opened it to find a picture of a very beautiful woman. She looked to be around twenty-four, with dark, sultry eyes and full, shapely lips. Then there was her mass of copper-brown spiral curls that flowed to her shoulders, crowning a cocoa-colored face. A pair of dangling gold ear-rings hung from her ears and a golden pendant necklace hung around her neck.

He knew he was spending too much time studying her features, but it couldn't be helped. The woman was strikingly beautiful.

Reluctantly he moved his gaze away from her face to check out the background of the photo. From the tropical vegetation captured by the photographer, she seemed to be on an island somewhere. She stood near a body of water that showed in the corner of the eight-by-ten photo. Scribbled across the bottom were the words:

Miss you, Godpop 1
Love, Swan

Swan? It was an unusual name, but it fit.

He moved to the next document in the file. Attached to it was a small family photo that showed a tall Caucasian man with sandy-brown hair and brown eyes standing beside a beautiful woman who closely resembled Swan. Her mother. In front of the couple was a beautiful little girl who looked to be around eight.

Flipper studied the child's face and knew that child had grown up to be the gorgeous woman in the first photo. The shape of her face was the same, as were her eyes. Even as a child, she'd had long curly hair.

The family photo was clipped to a profile of the young woman. As he'd guessed, she was twenty-four. Her name was Swan Jamison. She was an American, born in Key West. Presently, she owned a jewelry store on the island. That was all the information the document provided.

Flipper lifted his gaze to find his commanding officer and the admiral staring at him. "I assume this is the person naval intelligence believes is the traitor."

"Yes," Admiral Martin said. "She's my goddaughter. I am Godpop 1."

"She's my goddaughter as well," added Commanding Officer Shields. "I am Godpop 2."

Flipper's gaze moved from one man to the other. "I see, sirs."

Admiral Martin nodded. "Her father was part

of our SEAL team and our best friend. His name was Andrew Jamison."

Flipper had heard that Commanding Officer Shields and Admiral Martin were part of the same SEAL team a number of years ago.

"Andrew was the best. He lost his life saving ours," said Commanding Officer Shields. "He didn't die immediately, and before he died, he made us promise to look after his wife, Leigh, and his daughter, Swan." The man paused and then said, "Over twenty-eight years ago, when we were taking some R & R in Jamaica, Andrew met Leigh, who was a Jamaican model. They married a year later, and he moved her to Key West, where our team was stationed. After Andrew was killed, Leigh returned to Jamaica. When Swan graduated from high school, she returned to the Keys and moved into her parents' home."

"How old was she when her father was killed?" Flipper asked.

"She was fifteen," Admiral Martin said. "Swan was close to her dad. Leigh was so broken up over Andrew's death that she didn't want to live in the

States without him, which was why she returned to Jamaica. She passed away two years ago."

Flipper's commanding officer then took up the tale. "Leigh sent for us before she died of stomach cancer, asking us to look out for Swan after she was gone. We would have done that anyway, since we always kept in touch with both Leigh and Swan. In fact, Swan rotated summers with us and our families even after Leigh returned to Jamaica. We took our roles as godfathers seriously. We were even there when Swan graduated from high school and college."

"Did Swan have any American grandparents?" Flipper asked.

He saw both men's lips tighten into frowns. "Yes. However, her paternal grandparents didn't approve of their son's marriage to Leigh," said Commanding Officer Shields.

"So they never accepted their granddaughter." It was more of a statement than a question.

"No, they never did," Admiral Martin confirmed. As if it was a topic he'd rather change, the man added, "We've been given some time to find out the truth, but not much. Luckily, Swan's Godpop 3 has a high-level position at naval intelligence. Otherwise, we wouldn't know about the investigation. We have thirty days to prove Swan is not a traitor and identify the person who is. That's where we need your help. Instead of releasing you to go home as we're doing for the other members of your team, we are assigning you to a special mission, Lieutenant Holloway. You are being sent to Key West."

One

Key West, Florida

Swan Jamison was beside herself with excitement as she opened the huge box on her desk. Although it contained only her jewelry-making supplies, the package served as affirmation that while rebuilding was still taking place in certain areas, the majority of the island had recovered from the hurricane that had hit eight months ago.

"Anything for me?" Rafe asked, sticking his head through the office door.

Her shop was in a very trendy area so she could

capitalize on the tourists visiting the island. To help with high operating costs, she leased out one of the large rooms in the back. Rafe was her tenant, who'd converted the back room into a tattoo shop. On some days, he got more customers than she did.

"Nothing for you, Rafe, just supplies for me." She checked her watch. "You're early today." Usually he didn't open up until noon.

"I have a special appointment at ten thirty and I need to ready my ink." And then he was gone. Rafe didn't say a whole lot except to his customers.

The door chime alerted her that *she* had a customer. Jamila, who worked part-time and usually only in the mornings, had taken time off for a day of beauty—hair, nails, pedicure, bikini wax, the works. Her boyfriend worked on a cruise ship that was due in port tomorrow. Swan was happy for Jamila and happy for herself as well. The cruise ships always brought in tourists who wanted to purchase authentic handmade jewelry.

She walked out of her office as a man perused

her jewelry display case near the door. That was good. While he checked out her jewelry, she would check him out.

He had a nice profile. Tall, broad shoulders that looked good in a T-shirt and a pair of muscular thighs that fit well in his jeans. He had diamond-blond hair that was neatly trimmed and his hands were the right size for his body.

There was something about the way he stood, straight and tall, that all but spelled out *military man*. And the way his legs were braced apart, as if he had to maintain his balance even on land, spelled out *navy*.

Too bad. She didn't do military men. In all honesty, lately she hadn't done men at all. Too busy.

And then there was the issue of Candy's divorce. Swan knew she shouldn't let what had happened to her best friend darken her own view, but Swan was known to claim whatever excuse suited her and that one did at the moment.

And speaking of the moment, she had looked her fill. She needed to make her first sale of the day. "May I help you?"

He turned and looked at her, and every cell in her body jolted to attention.

Wow! She'd seen blue eyes before, but his were a shade she'd never seen. They were laser blue; the intense sharpness of the pupils captured her within their scope. And his features… Lordy! The man had such gorgeous bone structure! There was no way a woman had ever passed by him and not taken a second look. Even a third, while wiping away drool.

"Yes, you can help me."

And why did he have to sound so good, too? The sound of his voice—a deep, husky tone—made her throat go dry.

"All right," she said, walking over to him. She knew she had to get a grip. Her store had been closed for two months due to the hurricane, and now that the tourists were returning, she needed to catch up on sales.

"And how can I help you?" She didn't miss the way he was looking at her. She saw interest in his eyes. There was nothing wrong with that. She took pride in her appearance because she had been raised to do so. Leigh Rutledge Jamison, who'd been a Jamaican model, had taught her daughter that your appearance was everything.

Pain settled in Swan's heart. She missed her mom so much.

"I'm looking for a gift for someone."

Swan nodded as she came to stand beside him. Not only did he look good and sound good, but he smelled good as well. She glanced down at his hand and didn't see a wedding ring. He was probably buying a gift for his girlfriend or soon-to-be fiancée.

"What do you have in mind?"

"What do you suggest?" he asked her.

"Well, it depends," she said, looking into those gorgeous eyes.

"On what?"

"What the person likes. I make jewelry from stones, but as you can see, there are a number of them, in various shades, colors and styles."

He smiled and Swan felt a tingling in the pit of her stomach when a dimple appeared in one of his cheeks. "I honestly don't know what she likes.

Her tastes change from year to year. It's hard to keep up."

Swan nodded. "Oh. Sounds like the two of you have known each other for a while."

His smile widened even more. "We have. I would have to say I've known Mom all my life."

"Your mom?"

"Yes. Her birthday is next month. I was passing by your shop and thought I would drop in to see what you had."

A racing heart for starters, Swan thought. So the woman he was thinking about buying jewelry for was his mother. "Well, I'm glad you came in. Let me show you what I have."

"All right. There looks to be a lot of nice pieces."

She appreciated the compliment. "Thanks. I made most of them myself."

"Really? Which ones?"

She led him to the area set aside for Swan Exclusives. "These. Most of the stones come from India, Argentina and Africa."

He leaned in to look. "You did an excellent job."

Whoever said flattery, especially coming from a

good-looking man, would get you anywhere knew just what they were talking about. "Thank you."

"I'm David, by the way. David Holloway." He offered her his hand.

She took it and tried to ignore the sensations that suddenly flowed through her from the contact. "Nice to meet you, David." She quickly released his hand. "And I'm Swan."

"The name of the shop."

"Yes."

"It's a unique name."

"Yes, my parents thought so. On their first date, my father flew Mom from Jamaica to New York to see *Swan Lake*."

"Some date."

"Yes, he was trying to impress her."

"I take it he did."

Swan chuckled. "Yes, because he actually flew them there. He had his pilot's license."

"Now I'm impressed."

She didn't like bragging about her father but there were times when she just couldn't help it. "He served in the air force—that's where he learned to fly. And then he went into the navy after deciding he wanted to be a SEAL. That's when he met Mom, while he was a SEAL. She hadn't known about his stint in the air force until the night he rented a plane to fly them to New York."

Why was she telling him all this? Usually she wasn't chatty. "What about this one?" she asked as they moved to another glass case. "I call this piece *Enchantment*."

"Why?"

"Look at it," she suggested, leaning closer to the glass. He followed suit. "This is one of my favorite pieces because the teardrop gemstone necklace is pretty similar to my very first piece." No need to tell him that she'd made that one for her own mother.

"It is beautiful."

Something in his tone made her glance over at him, and she found him staring at her and not at the jewelry in the case. His eyes held her captive and their gazes met for a minute too long before she broke eye contact with him.

She swallowed. "So are you interested…in this piece?" She wanted to ignore the way her stomach seemed to be filled with all kinds of sensations, but she could not.

"I'm interested in a lot of pieces, Swan, but I'll start with this one."

Swan Jamison was even more beautiful than the photograph he'd seen last week.

The photographer hadn't fully captured the rich creaminess of her skin. And the shade of red lipstick she wore today seemed to make her lips plumper, more well-defined. Luscious.

He had read the dossier on her. He knew his commanding officer and Admiral Martin were operating based on a personal connection with her. He was not. If Miss Jamison was guilty of any wrongdoing, he would find out. And if she wasn't the one handing out classified data to China, then he would discover who was.

"So you want to buy this particular piece?"

Her question brought his thoughts back to the present. "Yes."

"Wonderful. I think your mother will like it."

"I'm sure she will. What about earrings?"

She lifted a brow. "Earrings?"

"Yes. Do earrings come with the necklace?"

"No, but I can make you some."

He'd been hoping she'd say that. "When?"

"It will take me a couple of days. The cruise ship docks tomorrow, so the shop will be busy. Two days from now will work for me, unless you need them sooner."

"No, I can wait. My mother's birthday is next month."

He would have an excuse to return to her shop.

Flipper watched her open the case and pull out the necklace. He knew his mother was going to love it.

"If you don't mind, please complete this ticket," she said. "And I will need full payment for the earrings before I make them."

"That's no problem," he said, taking the document from her.

After he completed the form, he handed it back to her. She glanced at it. "So you're from Texas?"

"Yes. Dallas. Ever been there?"

"Yes, once. I thought it was a nice city."

"It is. I was born and raised there."

"And what brought you to Key West?" she asked him.

"Work, at least for the next thirty days." That wasn't a total lie.

"Hurricane relief?"

"Something like that."

"You're military?"

"At one point but not now." He would let her think he was no longer military.

"I knew immediately."

He lifted a brow. "How?"

She shrugged. "Military men are easily recognized, at least by me."

"Because your dad is military?"

"He *was* military. Dad died years ago in the line of duty."

"I'm sorry." Flipper was always sorry whenever a fellow soldier lost their life.

"Thank you. Your package will be ready in two days, David. Your mobile number is on the form you completed. If I get to it sooner, I will call you."

"Two days is fine. I'll be back."

"'Bye, David."

"'Bye, Swan." He then turned and walked out of the shop.

As much as he wanted to invite her out to lunch today, he knew he couldn't rush things. He needed to earn her trust, even though he had less than thirty days to prove her innocence and determine who had no qualms about making her look guilty.

Swan was cheerful that night as she let herself into her home. Sales today had been better than normal. A tour group from New York had converged on the island and they'd come to spend money. She'd been happy to oblige.

Opening a jewelry shop had been a risky business move, but one that had paid off. She'd earned a degree in business management from the University of Miami and returned to the island after college to work as a manager at one of the elite hotels on the island. She'd enjoyed her job but had felt something was missing in her life. She hadn't been using her jewelry-making talent.

She'd promised her mother on her deathbed that she would find a way to use that talent.

Even after taking care of all her mother's funeral expenses, there had been more than enough money left to buy a little storefront. It had been a good investment because of its location. Some days were busier than others. This had been one of those busy days.

Now she was ready to wind down for the evening. She pulled her hair back in a ponytail and eased her feet into her favorite flats before heading to the kitchen for a glass of wine. As she did so, she couldn't help but think about her first customer of the day.

David Holloway.

He was a cutie, she had to give him that. And the memory of those eyes had stayed with her most of the day.

David Holloway had come into her shop to buy a birthday gift for his mother. How sweet. His mother was lucky. A lot of men didn't even remember their mothers' birthdays. She'd dated quite a few of those men and never developed lasting relationships with any of them. She figured if a man didn't treat his mother right, then there was no hope for a girlfriend.

As she opened the French doors to step out on the patio, she again remembered those blue eyes and how she'd felt whenever she'd looked into them. No man's eyes had ever made her feel that way before.

The effect was unsettling.

Okay, so what was wrong with her? Cutie or no cutie, she normally didn't get caught up over a man. She dated when it suited her, but she would admit that no one had suited her lately. At least not since her best friend, Candy, had left Key West to go live in Boston. Candy had refused to live on the island with her ex and his new wife— the one he'd married before the ink had even dried on the divorce papers.

Refusing to dwell on how shabbily Donald Knoll had treated Candy, Swan looked out at the water. It was calm tonight. When she had evacuated due to the hurricane, she hadn't known what to expect when she returned. Between her home and her shop, there had been some damage, but not as much as she'd feared.

The thought of losing her home had been devastating. This was where her father had brought her mom after they'd married. This home held so many childhood memories—of her father leaving on his missions as a Navy SEAL, of how happy she and her mother would be whenever he returned.

But then he hadn't returned.

Swan felt a knot in her throat as she recalled that day. She'd never seen that sparkle in her mother's eyes again. Swan recalled her mother telling her once that when you met a man who could put that sparkle in your eyes, then you knew he was a keeper.

Swan often wondered if she would ever find her keeper.

She had plenty of time. Besides, she needed to rethink her opinion about men first. If what Don had done to Candy wasn't enough to keep her single, all Swan had to do was remember William Connors, the businessman she had met while working at the hotel.

At the time, he had convinced her he was a bachelor without a care in the world but claimed that he wanted to make her Mrs. William Connors one day.

For some reason, Candy hadn't trusted him. She had a friend who worked for a private investigator check him out. Swan had been devastated when the investigation revealed there was already a Mrs. William Connors, along with three Connors children.

William had been playing her. He had been a lesson well learned. Her only regret was that she'd shared her body with him. She'd been young, naive and impressionable. He had been her first and he should not have been.

She was not naive now and she went into relationships with caution and even a little mistrust. Her mother once told her that being mistrustful wasn't a good thing. Swan knew she would have to learn how to trust again.

She took another sip of wine. Unfortunately, she hadn't gotten there yet.

"So how did things go, Flipper?"

"Have you met her yet?"

"Does she have a traitorous face or just a pretty one?"

"Do you think you'll be able to prove she's innocent?"

Flipper heard the questions coming at him nearly all at once. While unpacking, he had placed his mobile call on speaker to engage in a five-way conversation with his SEAL teammates.

"I think things went rather well, Mac. And yes, I met Swan Jamison today, Viper. I went into her jewelry store to purchase Mom a birthday gift."

Flipper eased open the dresser drawers to place his T-shirts inside. "She doesn't have a traitorous face or just a pretty one, Coop. The woman is simply gorgeous. Beautiful beyond belief. And yes, I hope to prove she's innocent, Bane, because Commanding Officer Shields and Admiral Martin truly believe she is."

"What do you believe?" Viper asked.

Flipper leaned against the dresser for a minute and thought about Viper's question. "Too early to tell."

"Did you ask her out on a date?" Coop wanted to know. They could hear Coop's two-year-old son, Laramie, chattering in the background.

"No, not yet." Flipper's attraction to her had been instant. He'd felt it the moment he looked into her face. Discussing her now wasn't helping matters. All it did was force him to recall what a beautiful woman she was—a woman he would have to spend time with in order to discover the truth.

"Then how do you plan to see her again if you don't ask her out?" Mac wanted to know, interrupting Flipper's thoughts.

"I ordered a pair of earrings to go with the necklace I bought for Mom. She has to make the earrings and I'll make my move when I pick up my purchases in two days."

"And if she turns you down?" Viper asked.

"Not an option. I now have less than thirty days to get this all straightened out."

"We should be there with you, watching your back," Bane said.

"No, you guys are just where you need to be, which is home with your families. I've got this."

"Well, some of our families don't appreciate us being home," Mac grumbled.

Flipper rolled his eyes. They'd all heard the complaints from Mac before. After every extended mission, their teammate went home to an adjustment period, where he would have to get to know his wife all over again and reclaim his position as head of the house. Sometimes the adjustment didn't go over well. Mac had a strong personality and so did Mac's wife, Teri. "Do we have to send both you and Teri into the time-out corners?"

"Hell, I didn't do anything," Mac exclaimed.

Flipper chuckled. "Yeah, right. You better get your act together, Mac. No other woman is going to put up with your BS."

"Whatever. So what did you notice about the place today?"

Mac was changing the subject and Flipper decided to let him. "Everything matched the architectural report I was given. Even with the repairs due to the hurricane, there were no major changes. Front door. Back door. High windows. Glass storefront. No video cameras outside. There are several rooms in back. One is being used as a tattoo parlor. I didn't see the person who runs it. I think I'll go out tonight and do a little more investigating," he said, sliding into a black T-shirt.

"Be careful, Flipper," Viper said. "Although you might not have seen any video cameras, that doesn't mean there aren't any."

"I know. That's why I'm wearing my Pilf gear."

Everybody knew how much Flipper liked digital technology. In addition to all the futuristic developments the military used, Flipper had created a few of his own high-tech gadgets behind the scenes. Some had been so impressive the federal government had patented them as Pilf gear to be used by the military. Pilf was the name Flip spelled backward. On more than one occasion, Flipper had been offered a position with the Department of Defense's Research and Development Department and had turned down each offer, saying he loved being a Navy SEAL more.

"We don't give a damn if you plan to parade around naked tonight, Flipper. Be careful."

He knew Mac was in his big-brother mode. "Okay, Mac. I hear you and I will be careful."

"Call to check in when you get back to the hotel tonight," Bane said.

"It will be late and I wouldn't want to wake up any babies, kids or a pregnant woman. I'll text everyone."

A short while later, wearing undetectable military gear under his clothing, Flipper left his hotel using the stairs.

Two

Two days later, Swan didn't leave the shop for lunch. Instead she accepted Jamila's offer to bring her something back from the sandwich shop on the corner. Although she'd tried convincing herself her decision to hang around had nothing to do with the fact that David Holloway would be returning today to pick up his items, she knew it did.

And her anticipation was so bad that every time the door chimed, her heartbeat would kick up a notch, only to slow back down when someone other than him walked in. She checked her watch.

The shop would be closing in an hour. What if he didn't make it before closing time? What if…?

The door chimed, and her heart nearly stopped when David Holloway walked in.

She'd told herself the man hadn't *really* looked as good as she remembered from that first day, but now she saw that he did. In fact, today he looked even better than she remembered. Maybe it had something to do with the unshaven look. Men with a day-old beard had sex appeal. But it could also be his tan, which indicated he'd probably spent the last couple of days lying in the sun.

If he'd been at the beach, there was a good chance he hadn't been there alone. But didn't he say he was in the Keys working?

Why did she care?

She quickly dismissed all those questions from her mind as she continued to watch him walk toward her in a strut that had blood rushing through her veins. His blond hair and blue eyes seemed brighter against his tanned skin. He was deliciousness with a capital *D*.

But then that capital *D* could also stand for *dan-*

gerous if she wasn't careful. Or it could stand for *delusional* if she didn't get control of her senses. Right now, she would play it safe and claim the capital *D* stood for *David*. She couldn't allow herself to think any other way for now, no matter how tempting.

She smiled. "Hello, David."

"Hi, Swan."

"Your tan looks nice."

He chuckled. "So does yours."

She grinned. "Yes, but mine's permanent."

"I know and I like it."

She didn't say anything to that because she understood what he was implying. He was letting her know he had no problem with interracial dating. She didn't have a problem with it either. Neither had her father, although his family had had conniptions about his marriage to Swan's mother. She pushed that thought to the back of her mind, refusing to dwell on an extended family that had never accepted her or her mother.

She reached behind the counter and retrieved a

box. "I hope you like the way the earrings came out." She opened it to show him the final earrings.

"Wow!" He ran his finger over the stone that came closest to matching the color of his eyes. "You're very gifted."

"Thank you, and I believe your mother will love them."

"I'm sure she will. I think I've outdone my brothers this time."

She closed the box and placed it, along with the one containing the necklace, into a shopping bag. "You have brothers?"

"Yes, four of them. I'm the youngest."

"My goodness. Any sisters?"

"Not a one. Three of my four brothers are married, so I have sisters-in-law. They are the best."

"And the fourth brother is still single?"

"He's divorced but has a beautiful little girl. And she's my parents' only granddaughter. They have six grandsons."

"Sounds like a nice family. Is your father still alive?"

"Yes, Dad is still alive. He and Mom own a medical supply store."

She nodded as she offered him the bag. "Here you are, David. Thanks again for your business."

He accepted the bag. "Thanks. Now that this is taken care of, there's something I want to ask you, Swan."

She lifted a brow. "What?"

"Would you go out to dinner with me tonight?"

Normally Flipper was good at reading people, but he was having a hard time reading Swan. He definitely needed to remedy that. Although both Commanding Officer Shields and Admiral Martin were convinced of her innocence, the jury was still out for him. He had to remain impartial and deal with the facts, not speculations.

For two nights, he'd searched the area around her shop. Getting inside without triggering her alarm hadn't been easy, but he'd done it. Once he'd picked up the location of the interior security cameras, it was a small matter to make sure he stayed out of their range and within a certain perimeter until he could deactivate them and do what he needed to.

"Go to dinner with you?"

"Yes."

She was apparently mulling over his invitation in her mind and he would give her time to do that. He had no problems studying her while he waited for her answer. Today she looked even prettier than the other day. He figured it had to be the lighting in this place.

"Yes, David. I'll go to dinner with you. You name the restaurant and I'll meet you there."

She wasn't going to give him her address and he had no problem with her being cautious. Little did she know he already knew where she lived and had visited yesterday while she'd been here at her shop. She had a beautiful home on the ocean. Inside it was as neat as a pin with no clutter. She'd even made up her bed before leaving.

"I noticed a restaurant off the pier. Summer Moon. I've heard only good things about it since I've been here." And he knew the place was within walking distance from her home.

"Everything you've heard is true. Summer Moon is fabulous and one of my favorite eating places. I'd love to join you there. What time?"

"What about seven? Will that be a good time for you?" He figured since it didn't get dark until close to nine, he wouldn't have to worry about her walking to the restaurant in the dark. After dinner, he would walk her home or put her in a cab regardless of the fact that she lived only a few blocks away.

"Seven is perfect."

"Good. I'll see you then."

Swan watched him walk out of the shop.

David had the kind of tush that made a woman want to squeeze it…after doing all kinds of other things with it.

She jumped when fingers snapped in her face. Frowning, she looked at Jamila. "What did you do that for?"

"To keep you from having an orgasm in the middle of your shop."

Swan rolled her eyes. Jamila, the attractive

twenty-two-year-old green-eyed blonde, evidently thought reaching a climactic state was that easy. "It would take more than ogling a man for that to happen, Jamila."

"I don't know. Your eyes were about to pop out of their sockets and your breathing sounded funny."

"You're imagining things."

"Denial can be good for the soul, I guess. So who is he?"

Swan and Jamila had more than an employer-and-employee relationship. Their friendship had started when Jamila first moved to the island a couple of years ago and patronized Swan's. It didn't take long to discover that Jamila liked nice things and decided Swan's was one of her favorite places to shop. Last year, Jamila had been looking for work after she lost her job as a day cruise ship captain.

As far as Swan was concerned, it hadn't been Jamila's fault when an intoxicated customer had tried coming on to her and she'd kicked him in the balls. Surgery had to be performed and the man had sued the ship company. They'd settled out of court but not before firing Jamila for all the trouble she'd caused.

Jamila had gotten an attorney herself so she could not only sue her former employer for an unfair firing but also sue the intoxicated customer. To avoid negative publicity, her former employer wanted to settle out of court with her as well. The intoxicated customer was also trying to settle since the woman he'd been with on the ship hadn't been his wife. If things worked out in Jamila's favor, she wouldn't need a job at Swan's much longer.

"He is a customer who came into the shop a couple of days ago to buy a gift for his mother."

"His mother and not his wife?"

"He says his mother."

Jamila snorted. "Men lie all the time."

How well she knew, Swan thought. Then she wondered why Jamila was men-bashing today. This wasn't the first comment of that type she'd made since arriving to work. Her boyfriend had come to town a couple of days ago with the cruise ship, right? So what was going on?

Swan decided not to ask. She didn't want to hear another sad story about a man that would ruin her date tonight with David. It was a date she was definitely looking forward to. She figured going out to dinner with him wouldn't be risky as long as she kept things in perspective.

She knew what could happen if she let her guard down when it came to a man.

Flipper deliberately arrived at Summer Moon early so he could see when Swan arrived. His stomach felt floaty the moment she turned the corner from the street where she lived.

Be still, my...everything.

She was wearing a printed sundress and a pair of high-heeled sandals, but what caught his attention—and was still holding it tight—were her long shapely legs that seemed to go on forever. He would love to see where they stopped under that dress. He forced that thought to the back of his mind.

But the closer she got, the more that thought wiggled back to the forefront. He shouldn't let it. He was on assignment and she was the subject of an investigation. He shouldn't see her as temptation. Letting his guard down around her could be a dangerous and costly mistake. He had to keep his head screwed on straight, no matter how innocent she seemed and how beautiful she was, and she was definitely one gorgeous woman.

Men, even some with female companions, were giving Swan second looks, and Flipper tried to downplay his anger. He had no right to be upset about other men checking her out when he was checking her out himself. The best thing to do to control his crazy reaction was to stop looking at her, so he glanced down at his bottle of beer and thought about the reports he'd finished reading a short while ago on her employee and her tenant.

Jamila Fairchild had worked for Swan for a year. He knew all about her former job as a captain of a day cruise ship, why she'd gotten fired and her litigation against not only her former employer but also the man who'd caused the ruckus in the first place. Naval intelligence hadn't left any stone unturned in Ms. Fairchild's report and she'd come up clean. Flipper would verify that she was.

Then there was Rafe Duggers, the tattoo artist. Although his parlor was located inside Swan's shop, there was a back door for his customers to use without entering through the jewelry shop. Flipper hadn't gotten a chance to look around the tattoo parlor and he intended to do another visit in a few days. Rafe was too squeaky-clean to be true.

No wonder naval intelligence was trying to point the finger at Swan. After all, it was her shop and they had somehow traced activity as originating there. But how? When? He hadn't found anything.

He had searched Swan's office, the small kitchen in the back, the bathrooms and another room that she used as a workshop where she made her jewelry. He'd come up with nothing, even after checking out her computer. So what were the grounds for accusing her?

Flipper's mind flicked back to Swan and he

stood when the waiter escorted her to his table. "Hello, Swan. You look nice."

"Thanks and so do you. I was trying to be early and you still beat me here," she said, sitting down across from him.

"I was thirsty," he said, sitting back down and indicating the beer. Now that she was here and sitting directly across from him, he was more than thirsty. If he wasn't careful, he could have a full-fledged attack of desire. She had a pair of beautiful shoulders and her skin appeared soft and smooth to the touch.

Then his mind drifted to wanting her and he quickly snatched it back. "You walked here. Does that mean you live close by?" he asked, deciding it was best to keep the conversation moving.

"Yes, not too far," she said. He knew she was deliberately being evasive.

The waiter handed him another beer and gave them both menus. "What would like to drink, miss?" the waiter asked her.

"A glass of Moscato please."

When the waiter left, she glanced over at Flipper before picking up her menu. "You're not working so hard that you're not enjoying the Keys, are you?"

"I'm doing a bit of both. I admit the ocean is beautiful tonight."

She smiled. "I think it's beautiful every night."

He nodded as he took another sip of his beer, straight from the bottle. "So are you a native or a transplant?"

"A native. I was born and raised right here on the island in the same house I live in now. My mother never made it to the hospital before I was born."

He raised a brow. "She didn't?"

"No. Mom came from a part of Jamaica where the belief was that when it comes to delivering a baby, a midwife is better than a medical doctor. My father promised to find her a midwife here. Otherwise she would have insisted that I be born in Jamaica and he didn't want that. He wanted me born in America."

"So he was able to find a midwife?"

"Yes, but I was born a few weeks early and the midwife wasn't here."

"So who delivered you?"

"My dad, with the help of three of his closest military friends. They were stationed at the base here and were visiting, watching a football game at the time. Needless to say, over the years I've gotten four different versions of what happened that night. My mother didn't remember a thing other than it took four men to deliver me. Although Godpop 1 claims my father passed out trying to cut the umbilical cord."

Flipper laughed. He then asked, "Godpop 1?"

"Yes, my father's three closest friends, the ones who assisted that night, became my godfathers. That's how I distinguish them. Godpop 1, Godpop 2 and Godpop 3."

Flipper nodded. No wonder the three men felt such strong ties to her. "You're lucky to have three godfathers. I don't have a one."

"Yes, I'm lucky," she said, after the waiter set the glass of wine in front of her. "They were my and Mom's rocks after we lost Dad, especially when my grandparents showed up at the funeral trying to cause problems."

Then, as if she realized she might have shared too much, she asked, "So what do you plan to order?"

Swan thought David had picked the right place for them to have dinner. When he asked for recommendations on what to order, she suggested Summer Moon's crab cakes and, as usual, they were delicious. The mango salad was superb, and after dinner they enjoyed listening to the live band.

When the band played their last song, she glanced over at David to discover him staring at her. The intensity in his gaze nearly scorched her and she took a sip of her wine. "Thanks for dinner, David."

"Thank you for accepting my invitation. The place is about to close. Are you ready to go?" he asked her.

"Yes." Because she knew he would suggest that he walk her home, she added, "If you still have a little bit of energy, I'd like to treat you to something."

He lifted a brow. "What?"

"A laser show that officially kicks off the summer season. It's a short walk from here." Since it was in the opposite direction from where she lived, she would have no problem catching a cab back later—alone.

He smiled as he beckoned for the waiter to bring their check. "Then by all means, let's go."

Once the show began, it didn't take Swan long to decide that David was wonderful company. She could tell he was enjoying the laser lights as much as she was.

She attended the event every year and it seemed the displays only got better and better. Each year, they honored a different state and tonight that state was New York. The New Yorkers in the crowd showed their happiness with whistles and shouting. And when a huge display of the Statue of Liberty flashed across the sky in a brilliant variety of colors, Swan caught her breath.

After that, the showrunners took the time to

honor the servicemen in attendance with a flag salute. She couldn't hold back her tears as she remembered how much her father had loved his country and how, in the end, he'd given his life for it and for her.

David must have detected her weepy state. He pulled her closer to his side.

"Sorry," she said. "I get all emotional about our servicemen and servicewomen, especially those who sacrifice their lives."

"You sound very patriotic."

She pulled back and looked up at him. "Of course I'm patriotic. Aren't you? You did say you used to be in the military, right?"

"Yes, I'm very patriotic," he said, wrapping his arms around her. She wished she didn't think the arms around her felt so strong and powerful.

"I thought you would be, but you said I sounded patriotic as if you thought that perhaps I wasn't."

"I apologize. I didn't mean it that way. I'm glad you're so patriotic."

She nodded, accepting his apology. Scanning the area around them, she said, "They are serving complimentary wine coolers over there. Let's go grab a couple."

"Sure thing." He placed his hand on the small of her back.

The contact sent a rush of desire through her that was so strong she had to force herself to breathe. Swan quickly glanced up at him and noticed he'd been affected by the feeling as well. However, he hadn't removed his hand.

Instead, he pressed his hand more firmly into her back and she felt him urging her away from the crowd and toward a cluster of low-hanging palm trees. Once they stood in the shadows, he turned her in his arms, stared down at her for a long moment and then lowered his mouth to hers.

The moment their lips touched, he slid his tongue inside her mouth, and she recalled her thoughts from earlier that day. He was delicious— and dangerous—with a capital D. And it wasn't just because he tasted of the beer he'd consumed at Summer Moon, but because he tasted like a hot-blooded man. All the sexiness she'd seen in him was reflected in his kiss.

When she began kissing him back, he wrapped his arms around her and deepened the exchange by crushing his mouth to hers.

She didn't mind his eagerness. In fact, she welcomed the pleasure of his hunger, his taste, which was getting more provocative with every stroke of his tongue. It had been a while since she'd been kissed, and certain parts of her were reminding her of just how long it had been. Not only that, those certain parts were goading her to keep up with the forceful demands of his mouth. She hadn't been kissed so thoroughly or possessively before in her life. Or so passionately.

Swan wasn't sure how long they stood there kissing. It wasn't until they heard the sound of fireworks that they disengaged their mouths. She glanced up as more fireworks exploded in the sky. Instead of looking up, David trailed his tongue along her neck and collarbone with wet licks.

"Say you'll go out with me again, Swan."

There was no way she wouldn't say it. She looked at him and saw deep desire in the eyes looking back at her. "Yes, I'll go out with you again."

"Good."

And then he lowered his head and kissed her again.

Flipper had tried everything possible to get to sleep. He'd counted sheep, counted backward, rolled his eyes for a full thirty minutes and had even tried hypnotizing himself. None of those things helped.

He couldn't remember ever feeling this tight with need. So here he was, close to four in the morning, and still wide awake. Nothing he did could erase the taste of Swan from his mouth and the act of kissing her from his mind.

The kiss would complicate his mission, but it hadn't been an act. It had been the most real thing he'd done in a long time. He had wanted that kiss. Needed it. It had been inevitable.

Sitting across from her at dinner and watching the movement of her mouth had caused a throbbing need to erupt in his gut, making him rock hard. There had been no way to ignore the delicious heat of carnal attraction spiking between them.

And the patriotism he'd seen in her eyes when she'd gotten teary-eyed in support of servicemen, and then when she'd told him about her work with the city to find lodging for homeless vets, hadn't helped. Neither had the fact that she'd looked stunning and had smelled irresistibly hot tonight.

Kissing her had made his entire body feel alive. Had revved up his passion to a degree that his libido had him tied in knots and had his pulse tripping. He could feel himself riding the fine edge of intense desire heightened by more sexual energy than he'd felt in a long time.

While kissing her, he hadn't cared that they could have been seen in spite of the low-hanging trees. He'd been beyond the point of caring. He'd been tempted to drag her to the ground right there.

Damn. How was he going to clear her of anything when the only thing he'd wanted to clear her of was her clothes?

He had access to women whenever he needed them. There were always women who went bonkers for men in uniform and he had no problem engaging in one-night stands. Those types of relationships had always been the way to go for him. He liked being single, coming and going as he pleased, with no one to worry about but himself.

It had been a long time since any woman had kept him up at night and that wasn't cool.

Grabbing his phone he texted the message: If anyone is awake. Call me.

Within seconds, his phone rang. It was Bane. "What's going on, Flipper?"

"Why are you up?" Flipper asked his friend.

"Feeding time. Crystal and I rotate."

"Oh? You're breastfeeding now?"

"No, smart-ass. The trio are on bottles now. What are you doing up?"

Flipper stretched out across the bed. "I couldn't sleep. I tried everything. I even tried to hypnotize myself."

Bane chuckled. "I guess it didn't work."

"No, it didn't work."

"So why can't you sleep, Flip?"

He wasn't one to kiss and tell, no matter who the listener was, so he said, "I still haven't figured out anything about the situation down here and the CO and the admiral are depending on me."

"Maybe they're going to have to accept naval intelligence's report that she's guilty."

"I don't think so." Flipper paused. "She cried tonight."

"What do you mean, she cried?"

"Today was the first day of summer and there's an annual laser show to commemorate the change in season. One of the laser displays was a salute to New York, where they did an awesome light replica of the Statue of Liberty and American soldiers. She got emotional and cried. Dammit, Bane, a person who is betraying their country doesn't cry for those in the service. Call me a sucker for tears but I don't believe she has a traitorous bone in her body."

"Then it's up to you to prove it. What about those two people who hang around her shop?"

"The woman who works for her and the tattoo guy? Both seem clean. But I will dig further. I have to."

"Okay, but make sure while you're digging for answers that you're not burrowing yourself into something you can't handle."

"What do you mean?"

"I think you know what I mean, Flip. You were sent there to prove her innocence—not to prove she has a passionate side. Remember that. Good night."

Flipper clicked off the phone and rubbed a hand down his face. Little did Bane know that after the kiss with Swan tonight, Flipper was driven to do more than prove her innocence, or her passion.

He wanted to possess Swan completely.

And he had a feeling the desire wasn't one-sided. He'd seen the look in her eyes during dinner. He'd felt how her body had responded to his touch. He was certain the same sensations that rushed through him had affected her, too. Kissing her had been inevitable, something they both wanted and needed.

The genie called desire was out of the bottle and Flipper honestly didn't know how to get it back inside.

Three

Swan pushed away from her desk and took another huge gulp of ice-cold lemonade. It had been that way for her all day. Instead of concentrating on the online orders she needed to fill and ship out, her mind was wrapped around that kiss from last night.

All she had to do was close her eyes to remember every single detail, specifically every sensuous lick of his tongue inside her mouth. Even now, the memory sent multiple sensations coursing through her body, causing pleasure the likes of which she'd never encountered before.

She looked up at the sound of a knock on her door. "Yes?"

Jamila stuck her head in. "Mr. Make-you-have-an-instant-orgasm is back."

Swan didn't need to ask Jamila what she meant or who she was talking about. "Any reason you can't wait on him?"

Jamila smiled naughtily. "I could use the pleasure but he specifically asked for you."

Swan nodded. "I'll be out in a minute."

"Okay, I will let him know."

Swan reached over and took another gulp of her lemonade. She didn't want to admit it, but after that kiss last night, David could become an addiction. Besides putting down a gallon of lemonade, she'd been twitching in her seat most of the day, thinking that if his tongue could do that to her mouth, then Lordy…she could only imagine what else he would be able to do…

She quickly stood, refusing to go there even as a naughty part of her mind wished that he would. Leaving her office, she rounded the corner and stopped.

David stood in the middle of her shop wearing a pair of khaki shorts and a muscle shirt. The sight of his muscled abs and strong legs made Swan bite back a groan. Just when she thought he couldn't get any sexier, he'd proved her wrong.

He must have heard the sound of her footsteps because he turned and smiled.

As if on cue, she smiled back. "Hello, David, you came to make more purchases?" Hopefully he would take the hint that she didn't expect him to just drop by without a reason.

"Yes. I'm buying jewelry for my three sisters-in-law and would love for you to offer suggestions."

Swan couldn't help but smile since she liked making sales. What store owner wouldn't? "I'd love to help you pick out pieces of jewelry for them."

An hour later, Swan stood at the cash register to ring up all of David's purchases. With her assistance, he'd selected some really nice pieces, with a number of the stones chosen specifically because that's what he'd said they would like. Then he wanted earrings to complement the necklaces,

which he paid for in advance. They decided to se-
lect stones for the earrings tomorrow since they'd
spent a lot of time on the necklaces today and her
shop would be closing in less than an hour.

From their conversation, she knew the Holloways were a close-knit family. He'd even pulled
out his phone to show her pictures of his young
niece and nephews.

"No pressure for you to marry?" she asked
when he tucked his phone back into the pocket
of his shorts.

"None. My parents have been married for more
than forty years and are still very much in love.
They make sure their kids and grandkids know
that. They believe we will know when it's time
for us to marry without any pressure from them.
We'll be the ones to have to live with the people
we choose. They just want all their children to
be happy."

She nodded. "I like the way your parents think.
I want to believe that, had my parents lived, they
would have a similar philosophy. Dad used to
tell me all the time that he wanted me to grow

up and be whatever I wanted to be and do whatever I wanted to do, and that he and Mom would always have my back."

She suddenly felt a deep sense of loss. "Appreciate your parents, David. You never know how truly great they are until they're gone. But in all honesty, I think I've always known I had great parents."

At that moment, he did something she wouldn't have expected from him—he reached out and took her hand. "They sound great and I know they're proud of your accomplishments."

"Thanks." That was a nice thing for him to say. To avoid thinking about just how nice he was, she slid the bag with his purchases toward him and gave him the credit card slip. He signed it and gave it back to her.

"How would you like to go to happy hour at Danica's with me?"

After talking about her parents and missing them like crazy, she could use more than just an hour of happiness. She would love to be able to have a lifetime of that feeling.

It wasn't that she was *unhappy*, because she wasn't, but there were times when she wondered if maybe there was more out there for her than what was currently in her life. Perhaps she was shortchanging herself on some things. What those things were, she had no idea.

"I would love to go but good luck getting a table at Danica's. They have the best hot wings and are always crowded, *especially* for happy hour. I think the entire island heads over there at five."

"Since I know you don't close your shop until five, how about if we meet over there at five-thirty? I guarantee we'll have a place to sit."

"Um, sounds like you might have connections, David Holloway."

"We'll see." He took the bag and turned to leave, and just like before, she watched his movements until he was no longer in sight.

"Wow. You do have connections, don't you?" Swan said, sliding into a stool at the bar. "I've been here a number of times and the best seat I've ever gotten is at one of those tables outside."

Flipper smiled. Like at Summer Moon, he'd arrived early and was waiting for her. He liked seeing her stroll down the sidewalk looking as beautiful as ever.

Today she was wearing a pair of shorts and a pretty top. Her legs were long and shapely and he could imagine them wrapped around him while…

Whoa, he didn't need to go there. Ever since that kiss, he'd been trying *not* to go there—no matter how tempted he was to do so. Quickly, he changed the direction of his thoughts.

"I know Danica personally," he said, trying hard to keep his naughty thoughts in check.

She lifted a brow. "Really? How?"

There was no way he would tell her the whole story. Danica was the godmother of former SEAL team member Nick Stover. Nick had given up being a SEAL a few years ago to take a job with Homeland Security after his wife had triplets. Instead of the whole history, Flipper gave her a modified version. "Her godson and I used to work together."

"Oh." The bartender chose that moment to take their drink order.

"I know you used to be in the military at one point but what do you do now?" she asked once the bartender had walked away.

Flipper had expected that question sooner or later and had a prepared answer. "I travel a lot and my job deals with ocean marine work. I guess you can say I'm a specialist in that area."

"Sounds interesting."

He chuckled. "Trust me, it is."

The bartender set their beers in front of them along with a huge plate of hot wings. They dug in.

"Your assistant at the store seems nice," Flipper commented. "I hope she didn't get offended when I asked specifically for you."

"No, very little offends Jamila, trust me."

"You've known her a long time?"

If his question seemed odd, she didn't mention it. "We met a couple of years ago when she moved to the island. The first time she came into my shop she nearly bought out the place. Like you, she has a huge family living up north and wanted to buy holiday gifts for everyone. Thanks to her, I made my month's quota in that one day. She earned a friend for life."

Flipper took a long swig of his beer. What Swan had just told him was interesting. Based on the naval intelligence report he'd read, Jamila didn't have any family. No parents, siblings, aunts, uncles or cousins. She'd been adopted and her adopted parents had been killed in a car accident in her last year of high school. And they hadn't lived in the north but out west in California.

Why had Jamila lied?

"So you hired her that day?" he asked, grinning, trying to make a joke of what she'd told him.

"No, she had a job as a ship captain at one of the day cruise companies in town. When things didn't work out for her there, I hired her on part-time."

He'd read the report and knew why Jamila had been let go and knew about her pending lawsuits. There was a big chance both cases would be settled out of court in her favor. "Is the reason she's part-time because she's a student?"

"Sort of. She saw how much money Rafe makes and—"

"Rafe?" He knew who Rafe was, but Swan didn't know that.

"Yes, Rafe. He rents space in my shop where he operates a tattoo parlor. He's good and always has a steady stream of customers. Some are so pleased with his work that they recommend him to others. I've known people to fly in just to use his services."

She took a sip of her beer, grinned and added, "Jamila decided to give him some real competition by becoming a tattoo artist as well. I have to admit she's pretty good. But Rafe doesn't seem worried. He even allows her to assist him sometimes. I guess you can say he's taken her under his wing. I think that's nice of him."

Flipper took another swig of his beer. "Yes, that is nice of him. Real nice."

Later that night, as they waited for a car at the taxi stand, Swan turned to face David. "I had a wonderful time this evening."

Once again, she had enjoyed his company and hated that their time together was about to end. It didn't come as a surprise to her that the sexual chemistry between them was more explosive than ever. The kiss they'd shared the night before had ignited something within her. From the way she'd noticed him looking at her, she believed something had ignited within him as well.

More than once, her smooth bare legs had brushed against his hairy ones. The sensual contact had sent a gush of desire through her.

The first few times it happened, she'd pulled away. But finally, she'd decided not to pull her legs back and he'd given her one of those *I know you did that on purpose* looks and she had smiled innocently and sipped her beer.

He had initiated the next physical contact and she could envision his mind at work trying to decide how to push her sensual buttons. She doubted he could push them more than he was already.

"I'm glad I got to meet Ms. Danica. After all the years I've been living here, this was my first time meeting her. She's nice."

"Yes, she is."

"And I definitely appreciate this," she said, holding up the bag of hot wings the older woman had given Swan to take home.

"I think she appreciated how much you enjoyed them."

She chuckled. "You're probably right."

"What do you have planned for later?" he asked in a deep, husky tone that seemed to have dropped a purposeful octave.

He had taken her hand when they left Danica's to walk to the taxi stand. The feel of his fingers entwined with hers had stirred something within her, something that grew with every step they took. She was aware of every detail about him as they walked together. Because of his long legs, more than once he had to slow his pace so she could keep up with him.

Swan could have walked home but figured he would suggest walking there with her. She was still cautious about letting him know where she lived. When she left Jamaica to begin living on her own, her mother had drilled into her the danger of letting a man know where you lived too soon. In her heart, Swan felt David was safe, but still…

"It's near the end of the month and I need to work on the books for my accountant." No need to mention she had tried doing that very thing today at work and hadn't been able to concentrate for remembering their kiss from last night.

"How about dinner tomorrow night?" he asked her.

She didn't answer right away. Instead, she broke eye contact with him and glanced down at the sidewalk. Hadn't they seen each other enough these last few days? Where was this leading? Wasn't he leaving the Keys in less than a month?

She glanced back at him. "Why? We've gone out twice already. I wouldn't want to dominate your time."

"You're not. And the reason I want to take you out again is because I enjoy your company."

She certainly enjoyed his. "Can I ask you something, David?"

He nodded. "Yes?" Considering her history with

William, it was something she probably should have asked David before going out on their first date. She'd discovered the hard way that a man not wearing a wedding ring didn't mean anything these days.

"What do you want to ask me, Swan?"

She met his gaze and hoped she would be able to see the truth in his eyes. "Do you have a wife or a significant other?"

Instead of guilt flashing in his eyes, she saw surprise. "No. I'm not married and I've never been married. I dated a woman for years but because of my frequent travels, she decided to end things. That was over six years ago." He then leaned against a light post and asked, "What about you, Swan? Have you ever been married or is there a significant other?"

"Of course not."

He nodded slowly. "Then I assume there is a reason you thought that maybe I was in a relationship?"

"I needed to be sure."

He didn't say anything. Instead, he looked at

her as if tumbling her answer around in his head. "But like I said, I assume there is a reason you needed to know."

"Yes." However, she didn't intend to go into any details.

"Well, rest assured there is not a Mrs. David Holloway out there anywhere. Nor is there any woman wearing my ring. Satisfied?"

"Yes."

At that moment, a taxi pulled up. "Thanks for dinner again." She was about to move toward the taxi when he reached out, took hold of her hand and tugged her to him. He lowered his mouth to hers and kissed her quickly but soundly on the lips.

"I'll see you tomorrow," he said, his words a soft whisper against her wet lips.

"Tomorrow?" she asked in a daze from his kiss.

"Yes, we're supposed to go over designs for the earrings, remember?"

It was hard to remember anything after a kiss like that. "Yes, I remember," she said.

"Then I'll see you tomorrow."

She nodded, and when he opened the door for her, she quickly got into the taxi and headed home alone.

The moment Flipper entered his hotel room he went to the small refrigerator beneath the wet bar and pulled out a beer. Just then it didn't matter that he'd already drank a couple at Danica's. He needed another. There was just something about Swan that was getting to him, touching him on a level he wasn't used to when it came to women. He had truly enjoyed her company tonight.

He and his SEAL teammates had just returned from a two-month mission in South Africa and more than anything he had needed to unwind. He would be home in Texas doing just that had he not been summoned to the admiral's office.

So here he was, and although he was in Key West on official military business and he was supposed to be investigating Swan, he loved spending time with her.

Tonight, when she'd met Danica, it had been priceless. You would have thought Swan had met a Hollywood celebrity. He had sat there while the two women conversed, immediately as comfortable as old friends.

The sound of Swan's voice had been maddeningly sexy with a tinge of sweetness that had stroked his senses. For the first time since returning to the States, he had allowed himself to uncoil, to loosen up and relax while appreciating the richness of her personality. Her persona was uniquely hers and the sensuality of her very being called to him in a primitive way.

And that wasn't good.

Taking a huge swig of his beer, he switched his thoughts to what he should be focused on—what she'd told him about Jamila and Rafe. Remembering what she'd said, he pulled his phone out of the pocket of his shorts and with one click he connected to his friend Nick Stover.

"This better be good, Flipper. Natalie is taking an art class at the university tonight and I have babysitting duties."

Flipper couldn't help but smile. Like Bane, Nick had triplets and from the sound of the noise in the background, the triplets had him. "Stop whining. Taking care of a trio of three-year-olds can't be too bad."

"Then you come do it."

"Sorry, I'm on assignment."

"So I hear. In the Keys, right?"

He figured for Nick to know that much meant he'd either talked to Bane, Viper, Mac or Coop. "Yes, I'm in Key West."

"While you're there, be sure to stop by Danica's. Give her a hug for me."

"I did that already. Tonight, in fact."

"Good."

"I think she has more photos of the triplets than you do."

"I wouldn't doubt it. So if you can't be a backup babysitter, why are you calling?"

"When you arrive at your cushy job at Homeland Security tomorrow, there are two people I need you to check out for me. I've read naval intelligence reports on them, but something isn't adding up. Call me a suspicious bastard, but after that situation with Bane, when those traitors within the agencies were exposed, I'm not taking any chances."

He then told Nick about the discrepancies between what the reports said and what Swan had told him. "Somebody is lying. Either Jamila lied to Swan or someone falsified the report, and I want to know which it is."

Four

"He's *baaack*," Jamila said.

Swan pushed away from her desk. She didn't have to ask who Jamila was talking about. "I was expecting him," she said in what she hoped was a professional tone. "He needs to look at designs for earrings."

"If you say so. I'll send him in here."

Swan was about to tell Jamila they could use the computer out front, but Jamila was gone after closing the door behind her.

Standing, Swan inhaled deeply. How she had finished the books last night, she wasn't sure.

Thoughts of David had been stronger than ever after their night out. When she'd gone to bed, she had dreamed about him. Okay, she'd dreamed about him before, but the dreams last night had been so hot it was a wonder they hadn't burned her sheets. She had been tempted to do something she hadn't done in a long time, reactivate her vibrator.

She drew in a deep breath when she heard the knock on her door. "Come in."

And in walked David, looking sexier than he had the other times she'd seen him. Last night, to stay focused, she had come up with every reason she could think of for why she shouldn't be attracted to him and why a relationship with him wouldn't work.

She'd even thrown in the race card. But of course that was thrown out when she remembered her parents and how happy they had been together. Yet she also couldn't forget how her father's family had ostracized him for his choice in love. Would David's family be the same way? There was no reason to think they wouldn't. And wasn't she getting ahead of herself for even throwing love in the mix?

"Hello, David."

"Swan." He glanced at her desk, taking in all the folders spread across it. "You're busy."

"That's fine. Besides, I need to get those earrings ready for you."

Now that he'd seen her desk, it would make perfect sense for her to suggest they use the computer out front to design the earrings. But now that she had him behind closed doors, she liked it.

Not that she planned on doing anything about having him here.

"Please have a seat while I clear off my desk." Today he was wearing jeans and she couldn't help but watch how fluidly his body eased into the chair. How the denim stretched across a pair of muscular thighs. She quickly switched her gaze before he caught her looking.

"Nice office."

"Thanks." She closed the folders and placed them in her inbox tray. She then glanced over at him and caught him looking at her. She followed his gaze and soon figured out why he was staring.

She was wearing a skirt with a V-neck blouse, and when she'd leaned over to place the folders in the tray, her shirt had shown a portion of her cleavage. Instead of calling him out for trying to cop a view of her breasts, the fact that he was interested sparked a distinct warmth between her legs.

She quickly sat down. "Now if you would roll that chair over here, I am ready." Too late, she realized how that sounded and quickly added, "To look at designs."

He smiled. "I know what you meant."

He rolled his chair behind her desk to place it right next to hers. When he sat down, their legs touched. Moving away would be pretty obvious so she let the denim of his jeans rub against her bare legs.

"Now, then," she said, trying not to notice how good he smelled. "What do you think of these?" she asked, bringing up a few designs on the computer screen.

When he didn't answer, she glanced over at him and found him staring at her. Sitting so close to him, she could look directly into his laser-blue eyes. It was as if his gaze was deliberately doing something to her, causing a surge in her breath and arousal to coil in her core. She saw the dark heat in his eyes and desire clawed at her even more.

"May I make a suggestion?" he asked in a voice that seemed to wobble in a sexual way.

"It depends on what that suggestion is," she heard herself say.

He leaned in a little closer and whispered, "I want to kiss you again. Only problem is that I don't want to stop until I get enough. And I'm not sure I would."

She had been staring at his lips, watching how they moved while he talked. She slowly dragged her gaze back up to his eyes. She saw need flare in his gaze at the same time that anticipation for his kiss thickened the air flowing in and out of her lungs.

"I don't know what to say."

"Don't say anything, Swan. Just bring your mouth closer to mine."

She knew she shouldn't, but she found herself doing it anyway.

Flipper drew in a deep breath when Swan's lips were almost touching his. He flicked out his tongue and she gave a sharp intake of breath when he began licking her lips from corner to corner with the tip of his tongue.

"What are you doing?" she asked on a wobbly breath.

"Since you asked…" He captured her mouth and when she closed her eyes on a moan, he reached up and cradled her face in his hands while he kissed her with a greed he didn't know was in him.

What was there about her that made him accept the primitive part of himself that wouldn't be satisfied until he made love to her? Was it because she crept into his dreams at night and into his every waking thought? Or was it because an arrow of liquid heat shot straight to his groin whenever he saw her? Or could he blame it on the fact that whenever she touched him, he burned? She made him edgy and aroused him as no other woman could.

It was all of those things and more.

Right now, he didn't know how to back away. So he didn't. Instead he accepted the stream of heat in his gut and the crackle of energy passing between them.

Their lips were copulating in a way that sent blood coursing through his veins like a raging river. It was raw, hot and explosive, causing a hot ache to erupt in his gut. It wouldn't take much to lose control and take her here on her desk. At that moment, his entire body was tight with need, totally entranced by everything about her.

The phone rang and they quickly broke off the kiss, drawing in deep breaths of air. He watched as she reached across her desk to press the speaker button. "Thank you for calling Swan's."

At first, no one said anything and then a deep male voice said, "Swan? Are you okay? You sound out of breath."

He watched as she pulled in another deep breath before a smile touched her lips. "I'm fine, God-pop 1. How are you?"

Knowing who she was talking to on the phone was like a pail of cold water drenching Flipper. He was quickly reminded why he'd been sent to Key West. His admiral would have him court-martialed if he knew what Flipper had just done with his goddaughter. If the man had any idea how many times Flipper had kissed her already and how each time he'd wished they had gone even further...

She turned off the speaker so he heard only one side of the conversation, and from the sound of her voice, he knew she was happy about receiving the call.

Feeling a tightness in his crotch from his still-aroused body, he got up from the chair and walked to the window. If she could have this sort of effect on him just from a kiss, he didn't want to think about what would happen if he were to make love to her. Just the thought of easing his body into hers had his stomach churning and caused an ache low in his gut.

Knowing he needed to think of something else, he glanced up into the sky. It was a beautiful day. Monday was Memorial Day and he wondered if Swan had made any plans to celebrate. He'd heard there would be a parade and unlike some places in the States, where stores remained open on Memorial Day, the laid-back businesses in the Keys closed up for one big party.

He liked the Keys. When he retired from being a SEAL, he could see himself moving here to live out the rest of his days. The island was surrounded by the ocean and they didn't call him Flipper for nothing. He loved water. Being in it and being a part of it. Living this close to the sea would certainly be a plus for him. But then there was the question of how he would deal with Swan if he chose to retire here. Even if he could prove she was not guilty of espionage, there was always that possibility she would hate his guts regardless of the outcome, because he had not been truthful with her.

"Sorry about that, David."

He turned, not caring that she could see his still-hard erection. It was something he couldn't hide even if he had tried. Was she sorry they'd been interrupted or was she regretting that they'd kissed in the first place? He hoped it was the former because he doubted he could ever regret kissing her. "I take it that was one of your godfathers?" he asked, knowing it had been.

She was staring at him below the waist, but after his question, her gaze slowly moved upward to his face. "Ah, yes, that was one of my godfathers. The other two will be calling sometime today as well. It always works out that they all call within twenty-four hours of each other."

He nodded and slowly walked back over to his chair to sit down. "I know you're busy so let's look at the designs."

Had he just seen a flash of disappointment in her eyes? Did she want them to continue what they'd been doing before she'd gotten that call? Didn't she know how close they'd both been to going off the edge and falling into waters too deep to swim out of? Even for him, a SEAL master swimmer.

Somehow they got through the next half hour looking at earring designs. Just as each one of the necklaces were different, he wanted the earrings to be different as well and reflect each one of his sisters-in-law's personalities.

When he was satisfied with his choices, he stood, convinced he needed to rush back to the hotel and take a cold shower. Sitting beside Swan and inhaling her scent without touching her was one of the most difficult things he'd had to do in a long time.

She was so female that the maleness in him couldn't help responding to everything about her. A part of him felt drugged by her scent and the intense physical awareness of her. Even now, desire was racing through his bloodstream.

"I owe you additional monies, right?" he asked. A couple of the designs he'd selected cost more than what she'd originally estimated.

"Yes. I'll let you know the difference after I

finish designing them, when you pick up every-thing."

He hadn't missed the fact that when he stood her gaze had immediately latched on to his crotch once again. Was she still hoping to see him with a hard-on? If that was true, then she wasn't dis-appointed. He could get aroused just from look-ing at her.

And why did she choose that moment to lick her lips? She had no idea that seeing her do such a thing sent the pulse beating in his throat and desire hammering against his ribs.

On unstable legs and with an erection the size of which should be outlawed, he moved around her desk and looked at her. "Yesterday I asked you to go to dinner with me again, but you never gave me an answer."

He figured that seeing how aroused he was, she probably wouldn't give him an answer now either. She surprised him when she said, "Yes, we can dine together this evening."

He nodded. "Okay, you get to pick the place."

She took a slip of paper off her desk, wrote

something on it and handed it to him. He looked at it and he must have stared at it too long, because she said, "It's my address, David. I'm inviting you to dine with me this evening at my home."

He broke eye contact with her to glance back down at the paper she'd given him. He looked back at her while trying to downplay the heat rumbling around in his gut.

"Do you need me to bring anything?" he asked her.

"No, just yourself."

Swan glanced around her home and felt the knots beginning to twist in her stomach. She hoped she hadn't made a mistake inviting David here.

Today marked a week since they'd met and if she was going to continue to see him while he was on the island, she couldn't take advantage of his thoughtfulness and expect him to invite her out without ever returning the kindness. However, more than anything else, she needed to keep things in perspective. She needed to remember he was someone she could have a good time with and that's it.

She didn't want anything more than that.

One day, she would be ready to explore her options and consider a future with a man, but that time wasn't now. She liked being single and responsible only for herself.

She knew from Candy that a serious relationship was hard work. And on top of all that hard work, you could assume you had the right person in your life only to discover you didn't. By then, you would have opened yourself up to hurt and pain in the worst possible way.

The thought that a man had caused her best friend that kind of agony bothered Swan whenever she thought about it. Candy loved Key West as much as Swan did, and for a man to be the reason she had moved away was disheartening.

Swan tried telling herself that not all men were like Candy's ex, Don, or like William. On days when Swan wanted to think all men were dogs, all she had to do was remember her dad.

Andrew Jamison was the yardstick she used to

measure a good man. She'd watched how he had treated her mother, had seen the vibrant and sincere love between them. She had not only seen it, but she'd felt it as well. Both her parents had been demonstrative individuals and Swan had often interrupted them sharing a passionate kiss or embrace.

She still felt it here, within the walls of her house and in the very floor she walked on. All the love that had surrounded her while growing up was in this house she now called home.

She was glad her mother hadn't sold it after her father died, when Leigh had made the decision to move back home to Jamaica. Instead, she had kept the house, knowing one day Swan would want to return. It was almost too spacious for one person but Swan knew she would never sell it or move away. This house had everything she needed.

She could see the water from any room, and at night, whenever she slept with the window open, the scent of the ocean would calm her.

Her favorite room in the house was her parents' old bedroom, even though she had not moved into it. It had floor-to-ceiling windows and a balcony she liked sitting on while enjoying her coffee each morning. A couple of years ago, she'd had the balcony screened in to keep the birds from flying into her house, although she loved waking up to the sound of them chirping every morning.

Although neither one of her parents would tell her the full story, Swan knew her father had come from a wealthy family. And she knew he had been disowned by them when he had fallen in love with her mother and refused to give her up. Before dying, Leigh had given Swan a beautiful leather-bound diary to read after her death. That's what had helped keep Swan sane, reading the daily account of her mother's life and love for her father and believing they were now back together.

For weeks following her mother's death, Swan had wanted to be alone to wallow in her pity and read about what she thought was the most beautiful love story that could exist between two people. Her mother had always been expressive with the written word and Swan enjoyed reading what she'd written.

It had made Swan long for such a man, such a love. Maybe that's why she had been so quick to believe in William and why, once she'd found out about his duplicity, she'd been so reluctant to get serious with a man since.

From her mother's diary, Swan discovered her mother's appreciation for her husband's agreement to make Key West their home. The people on the island embraced diversity and tolerated different lifestyles.

Swan had read the account of when her father had been stationed at a naval base in Virginia and had sent for her mother to join him there. In the diary, her mother had written about the hateful stares they would receive whenever they went out together. The unaccepting and disapproving looks. The cruel words some people had wanted them to hear.

Her father hadn't tolerated any of it and hadn't minded confronting anyone who didn't accept his wife. But to avoid trouble, Leigh had preferred to live in Key West, where people's issues with an interracial marriage were practically nonexistent.

However, people's attitudes never kept Leigh from leaving the island to join Andrew whenever he would send for her. Oftentimes, Leigh would take Swan along and they would both join Andrew in different places for weeks at a time.

When she heard the sound of the doorbell, Swan drew in a deep breath. The time for memories was over. The only plans she had for *this* evening were for her and David to enjoy the meal she'd prepared and later enjoy each other's company.

She had no problem with them deciding what the latter entailed when that time came.

"Hello, David. Welcome to my home."

Flipper pushed from his mind the thought of how Swan would feel if she knew this wasn't his first time here. How she would react if she knew he had invaded her space without her knowledge. If she ever found out the truth, would she understand it had been done with the best of intentions? Namely, to keep her from wasting away in a federal prison after being falsely accused of a crime?

He forced those thoughts to the back of his mind as he smiled down at her. She looked absolutely stunning in a wraparound skirt and yellow blouse. "Hi. I know you said I didn't have to bring anything, but I wanted to give you these," he said, handing her both a bottle of wine and a bouquet of flowers.

He had decided on the wine early on, but the flowers had been a spur of the moment thing when he'd seen them at one of those sidewalk florist shops. Their beauty and freshness had immediately reminded him of Swan.

"Thank you. The flowers are beautiful and this is my favorite wine," she said, stepping aside to let him in.

He chuckled. "I know. I remember from the other night." There was no way he would also mention having seen several bottles of Moscato in the wine rack the time he had checked out her house.

He glanced around, pretending to see her home for the first time. "Nice place."

"Thanks. I thought we would enjoy a glass of

wine and some of my mouthwatering crab balls out on the patio before dinner."

"Mouthwatering crab balls?"

"Yes, from my mom's secret recipe. You won't be disappointed," she said, leading him through a set of French doors. The first thought that came to his mind when he stepped out on her patio, which overlooked the Atlantic Ocean, was that it was a beautiful and breathtaking view. This had to be the best spot on the island to view the ocean in all its splendor.

He recalled how, as a boy, he would visit his cousins in California and dream of one day living near the beach. Over the years, being stationed in San Diego had been the next best thing. He owned an apartment close to base that was within walking distance of the beach.

However, his view was nothing like this. All she had to do was walk out her back door and step onto the sand. It was right there at her door. If he lived here, he would go swimming every day.

He glanced over at her. "The view from here is beautiful."

"I love this house and appreciate my mother for not selling it when she decided to move back to Jamaica after Dad died. She got a lot of offers for it, believe me. So have I. Mom said being here without Dad was too painful, but she knew I'd feel differently. For me, it was just the opposite. Being here and recalling all the memories of when the three of us shared this place makes me happy."

Hearing how the loss of her parents affected her made Flipper appreciate his own parents even more. Colin and Lenora Holloway had always been their sons' staunch supporters. Their close and loving relationships had been the reason none of their sons had had any qualms about settling down and marrying. All the marriages had worked out, seemingly made in heaven, except for his brother Liam's.

When Bonnie had gotten pregnant, Liam had done the honorable thing by marrying her. Bonnie had always been a party girl and didn't intend to let marriage or being a mommy slow her down. While Liam was somewhere protecting his country as a Navy SEAL, Bonnie was conveniently forgetting she had a husband.

No one, not even Liam, had been surprised when he returned from an assignment one year and she asked for a divorce. Liam had given it to her without blinking an eye. Since then, Bonnie had remarried, which had introduced another set of issues for Liam. He was constantly taking Bonnie to court to enforce visitation rights to see his daughter because the man Bonnie married didn't like Liam coming around.

Flipper had no qualms about marriage himself, but he had too much going on right now. Namely, resisting the temptation of Swan while he continued his investigation. That was his biggest challenge. The more he was around Swan the more he liked her and the more he wanted to prove her innocence. It was hard staying objective.

"Here you are," she said, handing him a cold bottle of beer. "I figured you would like this instead of the wine."

He smiled. Like he had picked up on her drinking preferences, she had done the same with him. "Thanks. I've never been a wine man."

She chuckled. "Neither was my dad. That's how I knew when it was time for him to come home because Mom would have his favorite beer in the fridge."

He opened the bottle, took a sip and noticed her watching him. He licked his lips, liking the taste of the beer, which was the brand he'd chosen the other night at Summer Moon. When he took another sip and she continued to watch him, he lifted a brow. "Is anything wrong?"

She smiled. "No, nothing is wrong. I just love to watch how you drink your beer."

He chuckled. That was a first. No woman had ever told him that before. "And how do I drink it?"

"First there's the way your mouth fits on the beer bottle. I find it very sensuous."

He tried ignoring the quiver that surged through his veins at the tone in her voice. "Do you?"

"Yes. And then there's the way you drink it like you're enjoying every drop."

"I am."

"I can tell." Then, as if she thought perhaps she'd said too much, she took a step back. "I'll go get those crab balls for you to try."

When she turned to leave, he reached out and touched her arm. He couldn't help it. The air all but crackled with the sexual energy between them. "Come here a minute before you go," he said, setting his beer bottle aside. "Although I do enjoy drinking beer, I've discovered I enjoy feasting on your mouth even more."

And then he lowered his mouth to hers.

Perfect timing, Swan thought, because she needed this. She'd wanted it the moment he tilted his beer bottle to his mouth and she'd watched him do so. And now he was doing her. Showing her that he was enjoying her mouth more than he'd enjoyed the beer. Just like he'd said.

There was a certain precision and meticulousness in how he mastered the art of kissing. First, as soon as his tongue would enter her mouth, he would unerringly find her tongue, capture it with his own and begin gently sucking in a way that made the muscles between her legs tighten. Then he would do other things she didn't have a name for. Things that made desire flow through her like sweet wine, kindling heated pleasure and burning passion within her.

He rocked his thighs against her and she felt him pressed against her. His arousal was massive. Instinctively, she moved her hips closer, wanting to feel him right there, at the juncture of her thighs.

When he finally pulled his mouth away, she released a deep, satisfied breath. Her mouth was still throbbing and there was an intense ache in her limbs. Right now, their heavy breathing was the only sound audible, and the laser-blue eyes staring down at her sent a tremor to her core.

She licked her lips when she took a step back. "Ready for a few crab balls?"

"Yes," he said, after licking his own lips. "For now."

Five

He wanted her.

Flipper knew he shouldn't, but he did. All through the delicious dinner Swan had prepared and while engaging in great conversation with her, the thought of just how much he wanted her simmered to the back of his mind. Now with dinner coming to an end, desire was inching back to the forefront. Images of her naked tried to dominate his mind, the thoughts made him shift in his chair to relieve the ache at his crotch.

"Ready for dessert, David? I made key lime pie."

Right now, another kind of dessert was still teasing his taste buds. "Yes, I would love a slice, and dinner was amazing by the way. You're a good cook. My mother would absolutely love you."

Too late, he wondered why he'd said such a thing. From the look on her face, she was wondering the same thing. So he decided to clean up his mess by adding, "She admires other women who can cook."

Swan smiled. "You don't have to do that, David."

"Do what?"

"Try to retract the implications of what you said so I won't get any ideas."

He *had* done that, but not for the reason she thought. He'd done so because it wasn't right for either of them to think something was seriously developing between them. More than likely, she would hate his guts when she learned why he was really in Key West, when she discovered she was his assignment and nothing more. He couldn't tell her the truth, but he could certainly set her straight on what the future held for them.

"And what ideas do you think I wanted to retract?"

"The ones where I would think we were starting something here, the ones that meant I would be someone you'd take home to meet your mother."

He sat down his glass of ice tea, which she had served with dinner. "Any reason why I wouldn't want to take you home to meet my mother *if* we shared that kind of a relationship, Swan?" Although he didn't think he needed to let her know—again—that they didn't share that kind of relationship, he did so anyway.

"Honestly, David, do I really have to answer that?"

"Yes, I think you do."

She stared at him for a minute. "I'm well aware when it comes to interracial relationships that not all families are accepting."

He chuckled. "My family isn't one of them, trust me. Interracial or international, we couldn't care less. My brother Brad met his wife, Sela, while working in Seoul, South Korea, and my brother Michael met Gardenia in Spain. Like I told you, my parents would accept anyone who makes us happy, regardless of race, creed, religion, nationality or color."

She didn't say anything to that. Then she broke eye contact with him to glance down into her glass of tea. Moments later, she raised her gaze back to him.

"My father's parents didn't. They threatened him with what they would do if he married Mom and they kept their word. They disowned him. Still, my mother reached out to them when Dad died to let them know he'd passed. They came to his funeral but had no qualms about letting Mom know they still would not accept her. They would only tolerate me since I was biracial. They even tried forcing Mom to let me go back with them. That's when my godfathers stepped in."

Flipper shook his head, feeling the pain she refused to acknowledge, the pain she'd obviously felt because of her grandparents' actions. But he'd heard it in her voice nonetheless.

"It's sad that some people can be such bigots. At the risk of this sounding like a cliché, some of my closest friends are black," he added, immediately thinking of Bane, Viper and Coop. Like her, Mac was of mixed heritage and had a white mother and black father.

"I'm sure some of your closest friends are, David."

He wondered if she believed him. One day, she would see the truth in his words. Then it suddenly occurred to him—no, she would not. There would be no reason for her to ever meet the four guys who were just as close to him as his biological brothers.

"I'll be back in a minute with the pie," she said. Then she stood and left the room.

Flipper watched her leave, feeling that he hadn't fully eradicated her doubts the way he'd wanted to do. That bothered him. He didn't want her to think he was one of those prejudiced asses who believed one race of people was better than another. What her grandparents had done to her father and mother, as well as to her, was unforgivable. Regardless of how she'd tried to come across as if their actions hadn't hurt her, as if they still didn't hurt her, he knew better.

She needed a hug right now.

He pushed back his chair and left the dining room to enter her kitchen. Instead of getting the pie like she'd said she would do, she was standing with her back to him, looking out the kitchen window at the ocean. And he could tell from the movement of her shoulders that she was crying.

"Swan?"

She quickly turned, swiping at her tears. "I'm sorry to take so long, I just had one of those miss-my-daddy-and-mommy moments."

He crossed the room to her, knowing that her tears were about more than that. He knew it and he intended for her to know he knew it. "Not wanting to get to know you—that was your grandparents' loss, Swan."

She gazed into his eyes and nodded. "I know, David, but their actions hurt Dad, although he never said it did. I knew. Mom knew, too. I think that's one of the reasons she loved him so much, because of all the sacrifices he'd made for her. That's why she did anything she could to make him happy so he would never regret choosing her. But it wasn't fair. He was a good man. Mom was a good woman. They deserved each other and should have been allowed to love freely and without restrictions, reservations or censure. It just wasn't fair, David."

And then she buried her face in his chest and cried in earnest. Wrapping his arms around her, he held her, leaning down to whisper in her ear that things would be all right. That her parents had had a special love, one she should be proud of, one the naysayers had envied.

Emotions Flipper hadn't counted on flowed through him as he continued to stroke her hair and whisper soothing words next to her ear. Inwardly, he screamed at the injustice of trying to keep someone from loving the person they truly wanted to love. It was something he'd never understood and figured he never would. And never would he accept such a way of thinking from anyone.

Swan knew she should pull out of David's arms, but found she couldn't do it. Being held by him felt good. His fingers, the ones that were stroking through the strands of her hair, seemed to electrify her scalp. They sent comforting sensations all through her—and something else as well. A need that he was stroking to fruition. As a result, instead of pulling out of his arms, she closed her eyes and enjoyed being held by him while inhaling his masculine scent.

She wasn't sure how long they stood there, but it didn't take long for her to notice his breathing had changed. But then so had hers. His touch had shifted from comforting to passionate. He was using the same strokes, but now the feelings within her were beginning to build to an insurmountable degree of desire.

Opening her eyes, she lifted her head to stare up at him. The minute she did, she caught her breath at the intense yearning she saw in his gaze. That yearning reached out to her, jolted her with a level of throbbing need she hadn't known existed. She'd heard of raw, make-you-lose-your-senses passion, but she had never experienced it for herself.

Until now.

"David…" She said his name as something burst to life in the pit of her stomach. It made a quivering sensation rise at the back of her neck. He implored her with his eyes to follow this passion, as if letting her know he understood what she was experiencing even if she didn't.

"Tell me what you want, Swan," he said in a deep voice while gently caressing the side of her face. "Tell me."

The intensity in his eyes was burning her, scorching her with the sexual hunger that was coming to life inside her. She wanted more than his erection pressing hard against the apex of her thighs. She wanted him on top of her. She wanted him to slide into her body and begin thrusting in and out. She needed to lose herself in more than just his arms.

Suddenly, she felt emboldened to tell him just what she wanted. "I want you, David. In my bed."

Flipper wanted to be in her bed as well. Lord knows he shouldn't want it, but he did. He would have to deal with the consequences later. He felt too tight and hot to try to fight the demands his body was making. Sweeping her into his arms, he quickly walked out of the kitchen and headed toward her bedroom.

"You think you know where you're going, David?"

He slowed his pace, remembering that she had no idea that he knew the layout of her home. Not only did he know where her bedroom was located, he knew the blueprint of the plumbing underneath her floor. He looked down and met her gaze, grateful she wasn't suspicious. "I figured you would stop me if I went in the wrong direction."

"Yes, I would have stopped you, but you're going the right way."

"Good." When he resumed his swift pace, it didn't take him long to reach her bedroom.

Swan had gotten next to him in a way he hadn't counted on happening. Seducing her had not been part of the plan and he should not have allowed things to get this far. He didn't want to think of the major complications involved, and not just because she was the goddaughter of three top naval officers.

But something was happening that he hadn't counted on. His mind and body were in sync and a rare sexual aura was overtaking him. He could no more stop making love to her than he could stop being a SEAL. For him to even make such a comparison was pretty damn serious.

Instead of placing Swan on the bed, he eased her to her feet, loving the feel of her soft body sliding down his hard one. "If you're having second thoughts about this, Swan, now's the time to say so."

She shook her head and then in a wobbly voice, she said, "No second thoughts, David."

Hearing her affirmation spoken with such certainty, Flipper released a low, throaty groan as he lowered his mouth to kiss her again, needing the connection of her lips to his as much as he needed to breathe. Wrapping his arms around her waist, he pulled her body closer to him as he deepened the kiss, wanting her to feel his erection, the hard evidence of his need for her.

He had never wanted a woman with this much intensity in his life, and he had no idea why Swan was having this kind of an effect on him.

Why she, and no other woman before her, had tempted him to cross a line during a mission. His mind didn't function that way. He had yet to prove her innocence, so technically, she was still naval intelligence's prime suspect, but at the moment that didn't matter. For all he knew, he could be about to sleep with the enemy.

But right now, that didn't matter either because deep down, a part of him believed she was innocent.

What was happening between them was definitely out of the realm of normal for him. He'd known he would have to get close to her, but he hadn't counted on this—his intense desire to do inappropriate, erotic and mind-blowing things to Swan Jamison.

But he wanted her and there would be no regrets. At least not for him, and based on what she'd just said, there would be no regrets for her either.

The moment he ended the kiss, his hands were busy removing her skirt, followed by her blouse, and when she stood in front of him in her lacy panties and bra, he couldn't help but growl his satisfaction. She looked sexy as hell and the rose-colored ensemble against the darkness of her skin was stunningly beautiful. *She* was beautiful.

He reached up and traced a finger along the material of her boxer-cut panties. This style on a woman had never done anything for him. Until now.

"You should have been a model," he said in a deep, throaty voice, filled with profound need and deep appreciation. She had such a gorgeously shaped body.

"My mother used to be a model. I was satisfied with being a model's daughter."

"And a strikingly beautiful one at that," he said, lowering to his knees to rid her of her panties. He couldn't wait to touch her, taste her and do all those erotic things to her he had dreamed of doing over the past few nights. He breathed in deeply, getting more aroused by the second while easing her panties down a pair of long, beautiful legs.

After tossing her panties aside, he leaned back on his haunches and gazed at her, seeing her naked from the waist down. Her small waist, her stomach, the shape of her thighs and longs legs were perfect. She was perfect.

After looking his fill, he leaned forward and rested his forehead against her stomach, inhaling her luscious scent. He loved the way it flowed through his nostrils, opening his pores and causing his body to become even more erect.

And then he did something he'd wanted to do since their first kiss. He used the tip of his tongue to kiss her stomach, loving the indention around her naval and tracing a path around the area. Then he shifted his mouth lower, licking his way down and enjoying the sound of her moans.

When he came to the very essence of her, he licked around her womanly folds before leaning in to plant a heated kiss right there. It was as if sampling her special taste was as essential to him as breathing. His hands held firm to her thighs when he slid his tongue inside of her, loving the sound of his name from her lips.

Then he went deeper, using his tongue to taste her, claim her and brand her. The latter gave him pause but not enough to stop what he was doing. He'd never claimed a woman as his own and had never thought about doing so. But with Swan, it seemed such a thing wasn't just desired but was required.

And he didn't want it any other way. She was the first woman he wanted to claim. Forcefully, he pushed to the back of his mind what it could mean to make any woman his and decided he would dwell on that aspect of things at a later time. For now, he wanted to focus on the delicious, succulent, enjoyable taste that was Swan.

He took his time, wanting her to know just how much he loved doing this to her. He wanted her to feel the connection his tongue was making with her flesh. However, he wanted her to do more than feel it, he wanted this connection absorbed into her senses, into her mind, into every part of her body.

Moments later, Flipper knew he'd achieved his goal when he felt her fingers dig into his shoulder blades, followed by the quivering of her thighs. Tightening his hold on her hips, he knew what would be next and he was ready.

She screamed his name when she was thrown into an orgasmic state. Her fingernails dug deeper into his skin, but he didn't feel the pain because knowing he was giving her pleasure made him immune to it. What he felt was a desire to take things to the next level, to slide into her body and go so deep it would be impossible to detect where his body ended and hers began.

He finally pulled his mouth away and looked up at her, saw the glazed look in her eyes. Without saying a word, he traced his fingers around the womanly mound he'd just kissed before inserting his finger inside of her. She was ultra-wet and mega-hot and he had every intention of capitalizing on both. The orgasm she'd just experienced would be small in comparison to the one he intended to give her.

Pulling his finger from her, he licked it clean,

knowing she was watching his every move. "Sweet," he said softly, holding her gaze.

He slowly eased to his feet and reached behind her to remove her bra. When she stood totally naked in front of him, he feasted his gaze on her. "And I'm about to show you just how sweet I think you are, Swan."

Six

Swan was having difficulty breathing and the blue eyes staring at her made getting air to flow through her lungs even more difficult. Never had she felt this energized from a sexual act. And when David got to his feet and leaned in to kiss her, letting her taste herself on his lips, she felt weak in the knees. But he held her around the waist, holding her up as he kissed her more deeply, making her wish the kiss could last forever.

She released a low disappointed groan in her throat when he pulled his mouth away.

"Don't worry, there's more coming."

He swept her off her feet and carried her over to the bed, placed her on it and joined her there.

"You still have clothes on," she said, reaching out to touch his shirt.

"I know and they will be coming off. Right now, I just want to lie here with you and hold you in my arms."

She smiled at him. "You're not going to fall asleep on me, are you?"

Chuckling, he said, "Asleep? With you lying beside me without a stitch of clothes on? Sleep is the last thing I'd be able to do, trust me."

He'd already pleasured her with his mouth, so she couldn't help wondering what was next. She soon discovered his intent when he reached over and cupped her breasts.

"You are perfect," he said in a deep husky voice.

The words triggered a memory of overhearing her father whisper the same compliment to her mother, after she surprised him with a special dinner after he returned home from one of his missions.

Swan knew she was far from perfect. Those

were just words David was speaking. But still, hearing them filled her with joy. Maybe she shouldn't let them, but they did.

Then any further thoughts dissolved from her mind when David eased a nipple between his lips. She moaned at the pleasure she felt all the way to her toes. Just when she thought she couldn't stand anymore, he began torturing her other nipple.

When he finally eased away, she opened her eyes to watch him undress. When he removed his shirt, she saw the tattoos covering his tanned skin on both of his upper arms—huge dolphins emerging from beautiful blue ocean waters. Another tattoo of even more dolphins was painted across his back in beautiful vivid colors. She'd never been into tattoos but she thought his were stunning.

"I like your tattoos," she said.

He glanced over at her and smiled. "Thanks."

When he lowered his shorts, her gaze moved to the area between a pair of masculine thighs. His shaft was massive and marvelously formed. Just the thought of him easing that part of himself inside of her sent her pulse skyrocketing.

"You okay?"

She lifted her gaze to his. She wasn't sure if she was okay. A thickness had settled in her throat when she saw how he was looking at her. Not only did he intend to join his body with hers, she had a feeling he planned to keep them connected for a while.

"Yes, I'm okay."

Swan continued to check him out, thinking he had a mighty fine physique. His body was all muscle and it was obvious that he worked out regularly. A man didn't get those kinds of abs if he didn't.

She watched as he pulled a condom from his wallet and sheathed himself in a way that was so erotic, she felt herself getting wetter between the legs just watching him. Then he was strolling back toward the bed. To her.

"I'm about to make sure you feel more than okay," he said, reaching down and easing her up to rest her chest against his. Her breasts were still sensitive from his mouth and rubbing them against his chest caused a multitude of arousing sensations to swamp her.

"What are you doing to me?" she asked in a ragged breath, barely able to get the words out.

"Anything you can imagine," he whispered, lowering her back on the mattress and then straddling her. He stared down at her as he gently moved her legs apart. She felt him, that part of him, lightly touch her feminine folds and then he was rubbing back and forth across them, sending even more sensations racing through her bloodstream.

"Trying to torture me, David?"

"No, trying to pleasure you. Ready for me?"

The movement of his manhood against her was making it impossible for her to concentrate. "What do you think?"

"You're wet and hot, so I think you're ready." And then he entered her in one deep thrust.

She gasped at the fullness and was glad he'd gone still for a minute. This gave her the chance to feel him fully embedded deep within her. It had been a long time for her and her inner muscles were greedily clamping on to him, tightening their hold.

"You're big," she whispered.

"You're tight," was his response. "But we're making this work."

And he did. First he began moving again, gently sliding in and out of her. That only lasted a few seconds before he picked up the pace and began thrusting harder.

She responded by wrapping her legs around his waist. Then he lifted her hips to receive more of him. When he established a slow and deep rhythm, touching areas in her body that hadn't been touched in a long time, or ever, she fought back a scream. She grabbed hold of his hair and pulled it, but he didn't seem to mind.

"Rule number one, Swan. Don't hold back."

Was he kidding? It wasn't a matter of holding back. It was more like she was trying to keep her sanity. David was so powerfully male that he was pushing her over the edge with every deep stroke.

Every cell within her vibrated in response to his precise thrusts.

"Hold on, baby. Things are about to get wild."

Flipper had given Swan fair warning. When he began pounding harder, making strokes he'd never attempted with another woman—going deep, pulling out and then going deep again—he felt a quivering sensation start at the base of his testicles and move toward her womb with each and every thrust. He had to hold on tight to her to keep them on the bed. He was determined to show her wild.

Simultaneously, he leaned down to have his way with her mouth, licking it corner to corner and then inserting his tongue inside with the same rhythm he was using below.

What he was feeling right now was more than off the charts, it was out of the atmosphere. When she finally let go and screamed his name, the sound vibrated in every part of his body, especially in her inner muscles. They clamped down on him, trying to pull everything out of him while her hands tightened even more in his hair.

"David!"

She screamed his name again. The sound drove him. He wanted more of her. Wanted to go deeper. Throwing his head back, he felt the veins in his neck strain. There was pain but not enough to dim the pleasure.

And he knew at that moment Swan had gotten under his skin in a way no other woman had.

He began rocking hard into her with an intensity that made him go deeper with every thrust. Then he was the one hollering out in pleasure, saying her name as an explosion ripped through him. Then like a crazed sexual maniac, he leaned in to feast on her mouth and breasts. It was like his desire for her could not end.

"David!"

He knew she was coming again and, dammit to hell, so was he. Marveling at such a thing, he tightened his hold on her. His control had not only gotten shot to hell and back but had died an explosive death as the result of the most powerful orgasms he'd ever endured.

This was what real lovemaking was about. No holds barred. No restrictions. Every part of him felt alive, drained, renewed. The room had the scent of sex and more sex. But that wasn't all. Emotions he'd never felt before touched him and swelled his heart.

He quickly forced those emotions back, refusing to go there. Knowing he couldn't go there.

The husky sound of deep, even breathing made Swan open her eyes. She was still in bed with David. Their limbs were entangled and his head was resting on her chest as he slept.

This man had been the most giving of lovers. He didn't come until he made sure she came first. He had kissed every part of her body, some parts more than others, and he had stoked passion within her in a way that had made her reach the boiling point. No man had ever made love to her with such intensity.

He had warned her about them getting wild. As

far as she was concerned, they had gotten more than wild, they had gotten uninhibited, untamed. She hadn't known she had so much passion within her. He had brought it out and made her do more than own it. He had made her so aware of it that she doubted she could undo what he'd done.

David Holloway had done more than push a few of her buttons. He had turned on all the lights.

That thought made her smile and pull him closer. Feeling exhausted, she closed her eyes and drifted into sleep.

Flipper slowly opened his eyes, taking in the sight and scent of the woman lying beside him, snuggled close to his body. He was so sexually contented, he could groan out loud. He didn't. Instead he tightened his arms around her.

Things had gotten wild. They had finally fallen asleep after four rounds of the most satisfying lovemaking possible.

While making love with Swan, he had discovered there was a vast difference in making love to her versus making love to other women. He'd known it before but she had made that point crystal clear tonight.

With other women, he'd usually had one goal in mind—seeking sexual pleasure and making sure she got hers. With Swan it had been about that, too, but it had also been about finding closeness. No other woman had made him want to stay inside her. It had only been the need to replace condoms that had forced him from Swan's side. And then he had been back inside her in a flash…like that was where he belonged. Hell, he was still thinking that way and the twitch in his aroused manhood was letting him know just what he desired.

Flipper was known to have a robust sexual appetite. When you lived your life on the edge, engaging in covert operations as his team did, then you needed a way to release.

Usually, unerringly, he found his release in some woman's bed. He made sure she knew it was one and done. Due to the nature of his occupation, he didn't have time for attachments or anything long-term. Some SEALs did; he didn't.

He'd tried it once and it hadn't worked out. Now he preferred being a loner. It didn't bother him that he was the lone single guy among his close friends. To each his own.

So how could one night in Swan Jamison's bed have him thinking things he shouldn't be thinking, especially considering why he was in Key West in the first place?

It had everything to do with the woman he'd had mind-blowing sex with for the past four hours or so. Now he saw her as more than an assignment. Now she was also a woman who had the ability to match his sexual needs one-on-one, something he found invigorating and energizing on all levels. He was a totally physical male and Swan Jamison was wholly, utterly female. Almost to the point that she'd blown his ever-loving mind.

Now she was sleeping peacefully while he was lying here thinking, knowing his honor was being tested. As a military man, he always did what was honorable. On top of that, his mother had drilled into all five of her sons that honor was not just for their country but extended to humans just as much, especially women. Why had that thought settled deep into his mind now?

One reason might be that he'd read the report on her. He knew about those elderly people residing at the senior living complex that she visited on her weekends off and how she'd championed so hard for the homeless. She was working with the mayor to help find funding to build a housing complex for them.

She was a caring person. He'd witnessed her love for her country, for her father, that night at the fireworks and the more he was around her, the more he believed in her innocence.

She made a sound now and he glanced down and met beautiful brown eyes staring at him. Immediately his senses connected with those eyes. She trusted him. He could see it in the gaze staring back at him. Otherwise he would not be here in her bed.

What would she think when she learned the truth? Would she still trust him? He pushed the thought to the back of his mind.

She gave him a beautiful, sleepy smile that

melted his insides. Made him wish he had come here to the Keys for a real vacation, a much-needed one. He wished he had entered her shop with no ulterior motive but to do as he claimed, which was to buy his mother a birthday gift. He would still have tried his hand at seducing her, but things would have been different. Specifically, he wouldn't feel as if his honor was being compromised.

"You didn't try my key lime pie," she whispered.

"We can get up and eat some now if you want," he said.

"No, I like being just where I am. We can always eat some later...or even for breakfast."

He leaned down and brushed a kiss across her lips. "Um, breakfast sounds nice. Is that an invitation to stay the night?"

"Only if you want to."

He wanted to. And when he brushed another kiss across her lips, he slid his tongue inside her mouth to kiss her deeply and let her know how much he wanted to stay.

He knew at that moment that his commanding officer and the admiral weren't the only ones with a personal interest in Swan Jamison. He now had a personal interest in her as well.

Seven

The next morning, Swan woke up to bright sunlight flowing in through her window and a powerfully male body sleeping beside her.

Last night was rated right up there with *Ripley's Believe It or Not*. It had been just that spectacular. They'd made love a couple more times before getting up after midnight to eat the pie she'd prepared for dessert. After clearing off the table and loading the dishes into the dishwasher, he'd suggested they walk on the beach.

So at one in the morning, they had strolled hand in hand along the water's edge. It had been a beautiful night with a full moon in the sky. The breeze off the ocean had provided the perfect reason for him to pull her close while walking barefoot in the sand. He told her more about his family; namely about his parents' medical supply company.

Then at some point, they began talking about her company and she found herself telling him just about everything about jewelry making. He was curious about her stones and complimented how beautiful they were and inquired how she was able to create so many pieces.

No man had ever taken an interest in her work before and she was excited that he thought what she did for a living was important. She had found herself explaining the day-to-day operations of Swan's. He couldn't believe how she found the time to handcraft a number of the items sold in her shop.

David also thought it was great that Rafe, through his connections with a huge distributor in California, was able to get some of Swan's more expensive stones at a lower cost and had even helped her save on shipping by including them in the packaging with his ink.

She glanced over at him now as he shifted in bed. He kept his arms wrapped around her while he slept. She studied his features and saw how relaxed he looked.

She drew in a deep breath, still amazed at the depth of what they had shared last night. It had been the most profound thing she'd ever experienced with a man. Making love with David had touched her in ways she hadn't thought possible. He had made her feel things she hadn't ever felt before and those things weren't just sexual in nature. While in his arms, she had felt safe and secure. Protected.

As far as she was concerned, what they'd shared last night was more compelling and meaningful than any other time she'd shared with a man, even more meaningful than the time she'd spent with William. She'd never really allowed herself to fully let go with William. Now she could admit to herself that she'd known in the back of her mind that something didn't add up with him.

Yet she'd been so desperate for companionship after losing her mother that she had wanted to believe William was honest, even though he'd seemed too good to be true. She was glad Candy had become suspicious when he'd never wanted them to be photographed together or when he'd insisted that they spend the night at Swan's place instead of the hotel.

At the time, his requests hadn't bothered her because she hadn't wanted her employer or her coworkers to get in her business. But Candy had seen through all that and knew something in the milk wasn't clean, as she would often say. It had been Candy who'd unveiled her own husband's secret affair with a flight attendant. And once confronted, Don hadn't denied a thing. He'd said he was glad she'd found out because he wanted a divorce.

Pushing thoughts of Don's and William's betrayals to the back of her mind, Swan continued to study David. She couldn't help but recall the number of times he'd made her climax. Now that was simply amazing all by itself.

She was enjoying her time with him, even knowing it wouldn't last. Later this month, he would leave the island and she would probably not hear from him again. She knew that, accepted it. She had long ago learned to live for the now and not sweat the small stuff. Especially those things she couldn't change.

"You're awake."

She couldn't help but smile at the slumberous blue eyes staring at her. The dark shadow on his chin made him look even sexier. "Yes, I'm awake. I guess I should be a good host and prepare breakfast before you leave."

"Um, I've overstayed my welcome?"

"No, but today is Sunday and I have a lot to do."

"Maybe I can help you."

"You don't know what I'll be doing."

He reached out and pushed her hair back off her shoulders so he could completely see her face. "Then tell me."

She gazed into his eyes. "The shop is closed on Sundays and I use my day off to visit Golden Manor Senior Place. My mom used to do volunteer work there when we lived on the island years ago. I would go with her on Sundays to visit everyone. I guess you could say it's become a family tradition that I decided to continue."

"I think that's a wonderful thing you're doing. I'm sure the residents there appreciate it."

"Yes, they do, although those who knew my mom are no longer there. They've passed on. I'm establishing new relationships and friendships."

"Good for you. I'd love to join you."

"You would?" she asked, surprised.

"Yes, and don't worry about preparing breakfast. I'll go home and refresh and be back here within an hour. We can grab breakfast somewhere before heading over. Afterward, we can spend more time on the beach. I enjoyed the walk last night with you."

And she had enjoyed it, too. The thought that he wanted to spend more time with her made her feel really good inside. "Okay, that sounds wonderful."

"I'm glad you think so, and before I leave…"

"Yes?"

He leaned over to kiss her and she knew where things would lead from there. She looked forward to getting wild again with him.

Flipper clicked on his phone the minute he walked into his hotel room. He noted several missed calls since he'd deliberately cut off his phone last night. One was from the admiral, who was probably calling for an update. But first Flipper would return the call to Nick.

"Flipper, should I ask why I couldn't reach you last night?"

"No, you shouldn't," Flipper said, flopping down in the nearest chair.

"You have heard the saying that you shouldn't mix business with pleasure, right?"

Too late for that, Flipper thought, running a hand down his face. Instead of responding to Nick's comment, he said, "I hope you have something for me. There's another angle I want you to check out."

"Okay, and yes, I have something for you. I found out the initial investigation was handed off to a group of civilian investigators, which means naval intelligence didn't rank it at the top at first."

Flipper was very much aware of the part government bureaucracy played in certain investigations. If someone thought a case should be under naval intelligence's radar, then they made sure it got there. "Why?"

"Not sure yet, but first, let's talk about Jamila Fairchild."

Flipper leaned forward in his chair. "Okay, let's talk about her. What do you have?"

"Not what you obviously think. What she told Swan was the truth. She does have a huge family who lives in the north."

Flipper raised a brow. "Then who made the error in the report from naval intelligence?"

"Don't know, but it's worth checking out, although I don't think it's anything suspicious on Ms. Fairchild's end. Especially when I tell you who her family is."

"And who is her family?"

"Her mother's brother is Swan's grandfather."

A frown covered Flipper's face. "The grandfather who disowned Swan's father?"

"Yes, from what I've gathered. But I can find no record of her grandfather ever reaching out to her."

"Interesting."

"Yes, it is. I take it Swan Jamison doesn't know about the family connection."

"No, she doesn't." Flipper decided not to try to wrap his head around this bit of news just yet. Instead he asked, "What about Rafe Duggers?"

"Personally, I think something is going on with him."

Flipper lifted a brow. "What?"

"First of all, certain aspects of his info are sealed."

"Sealed?"

"Yes. I would think if naval intelligence was checking into something related to Swan and her story, they would see that sealed record for her tenant as a red flag. For them not to have flagged it raises my own suspicions about a few things."

That raised Flipper's suspicions as well. Was

Rafe a double agent? Someone working under-cover? Was someone in naval intelligence delib-erately setting Swan up as the traitor? If so, why?

"You weren't able to find out anything about him?"

There was a husky chuckle. "I didn't say that. There are ways to find out anything you want when you know how to do it."

And Nick knew how to do it. He'd been an amazing SEAL, but as far as Flipper was con-cerned, Nick's natural investigative talents were better served at Homeland Security. "When will you let me know something?"

"Give me a couple of days. In the meantime, don't say anything to anyone about my suspicions about Duggers."

"Not even the CO and admiral?"

"Not even them for now. You mentioned Swan had a third godfather who was someone high up at naval intelligence. Was his identity revealed to you?"

"No, it wasn't but then I didn't ask," Flipper said.

"It wasn't hard to find out," Nick replied. "All

you have to do is find out who Andrew Jamison's SEAL teammates were at the time he died and do a little research to determine where they are now."

"I take it you've done that."

"Yes, and would you believe Swan Jamison's third godfather is Director of Naval Intelligence Samuel Levart?"

Flipper would not have considered Director Levart in a million years, but it all made sense now. In order for someone to have delayed making formal charges against Swan, that person would have to be someone in power. The admiral had alluded to as much. "Swan doesn't know how favored she is to have three powerful men in her corner."

"Yes, but we both know it wouldn't matter if one of her godfathers was the President. If naval intelligence believes they have enough evidence to prosecute her, they will," Nick said.

Flipper knew that to be true. Now more than ever he had to find the person intent on framing Swan. To him, it was beginning to look like an inside job.

"So what else do you have for me to check out?" Nick asked, reclaiming Flipper's attention.

"It's about something Swan told me." He then shared with Nick the information about Rafe Duggers's association with some huge distributor in California. "I need you to check that out."

"I will. I know time is of the essence so I'll get back to you soon, Flipper."

"Thanks, I appreciate it."

"If you're so concerned about me, then why not return to the Keys and keep an eye on me, Candy?" Swan asked. She moved around her bedroom getting dressed while talking to her friend on speakerphone.

"You know why I won't return, just yet. But I did hear something that's interesting."

"What?" Swan asked as she shimmied into her skirt.

"I talked to Francola the other day and she said Marshall mentioned to her that Don is thinking about moving away from the island."

Swan paused. Francola and her husband, Marshall, had been close friends of Don and Candy's while they were married. The two couples often did things together. Personally, Swan didn't care much for Francola because the woman had been aware Don was cheating on Candy but hadn't told her friend. "I would take anything Francola says with a grain of salt these days," Swan said as she continued dressing.

"I know you still fault her for not telling me about Don and I admit I was angry with her, too, but now I understand her not doing so."

"Do you?"

"Yes. Her relationship with me is not like our relationship, Swan. You and I have been best friends since grade school and we have no secrets. You would have told me about Don had you suspected anything."

"Darn right."

"Well, Francola and I didn't have that kind of relationship. We only met through our husbands, who worked together. Besides, I'm not sure I would have believed her even had she told me. I would have been in denial." Candy paused. "Now, enough about me. Tell me more about this David Holloway."

Swan smiled while putting hoop earrings into her ears. "He's a real nice guy. Thoughtful. Considerate. Handsome as sin." She glanced over at her made-up bed. Although there were no signs of anyone sleeping in it last night, it didn't take much for her to remember all the wild action she and David had shared under the sheets. "And he's great in bed. More than great. He's fantastic."

"Just be careful, Swan. Protect your heart."

Swan slipped her feet into her sandals. "My heart? It's not like I'm falling for the guy, Candy."

"Aren't you? I can hear it in your voice. You like him a lot."

Yes, she did like him a lot. "It won't go beyond me liking him," she said, trying to convince herself of that more so than Candy.

"Can you honestly say that?"

"Yes, because I can't let it. His work brought him to the island and he'll be leaving soon. In less than thirty days."

"Doesn't matter."

Swan knew for her it *did* matter. She only wanted short-term. The last thing she wanted was to do long-term with any man.

Eight

"I enjoyed my time with you today, Swan," Flipper said, looking down at her.

They'd had brunch at Summer Moon before heading to the senior living complex where they spent the next four hours. She assisted the staff by reading to groups of people and even taking a few of the seniors for walks around the complex. Some, she'd explained, had family who rarely visited so she had become like their surrogate granddaughter.

On the flip side, considering what she'd missed

out having in her life, he couldn't help but wonder if they had become her surrogate grandparents.

From the moment she walked into the facility, everyone brightened up when they saw her. It was amazing to him. She knew just what to say to elicit a smile or to get them to engage in more conversation. The majority of the seniors knew her by name and he couldn't help noticing a number of the women wearing what looked like necklaces she'd made.

When he inquired about the necklaces Swan confirmed they were her designs but she had taught the women to make them from stones she'd given them. It had taken longer than normal since a lot of the older women's hands weren't as nimble as they used to be.

After leaving the nursing home, they'd grabbed lunch at a sidewalk café before returning to her house where they'd spent the rest of the day on the beach. Later, after ordering takeout for dinner from Arness, they were back at her place.

No matter how tempting Swan was making it for him to stay longer at her place, he would leave when it got dark. The information about Rafe Duggers's sealed records bothered him and he'd decided to poke around in the tattoo parlor later that night to see what he could find.

He glanced over at Swan as she sat across the table from him eating dinner. Earlier today, when he had returned to take her to breakfast, she had opened the door looking fresh and perky and dressed simply in a pair of shorts and a tank top. Seeing her dressed that way reminded him of just what a gorgeous pair of legs she had, as well as how those same legs had wrapped around him while they'd made love that morning and the night before.

When they had gone swimming, she'd worn one of the sexiest two-piece bathing suits he'd ever seen. He had totally and completely enjoyed his day with her. They would be attending the Memorial Day festivities together tomorrow in town, which included a parade.

Because he needed some investigative time, he'd come up with an excuse for why he couldn't see her a couple of days this week. Time was moving quickly and he had yet to find anything to clear her of wrongdoing.

Because of Nick's warning, Flipper hadn't told Admiral Martin everything when he'd called him back yesterday. Namely, he'd left out the discrepancies between what Nick had found out and the actual reports from naval intelligence. Until Flipper discovered what was going on, he would follow Nick's advice and keep that information to himself for now.

"Although I won't be seeing you for a few days because of work, will you still be on the island?" Swan asked.

It was hard not to be totally truthful about why she wouldn't be seeing him. She was the last person he wanted to be dishonest with but he had no choice. His goal had always been to prove her innocence and now that was doubly true. He would check out the tattoo shop tonight and look around in both Rafe's and Jamila's homes this week while they were here at work. Although it had been established that Jamila was Swan's relative, as far as Flipper was concerned, she was still a suspect.

"Yes, I'll still be on the island but I have to concentrate on this project I was sent here to do." No need to tell her that the project involved her.

"I understand how things are when work calls."

He reached up and caressed the side of her face. "We still have a date for the parade tomorrow, right?"

"Yes."

"What about dinner on Friday evening?" he asked her.

Her smile touched something deep within him. "I'd love that, David."

"Good. I'll swing by your shop at closing time Friday and we can go to dinner directly from there. You pick the place."

"All right."

"What time do you want me to come get you for the parade tomorrow?"

"It starts at ten in the morning and we need to get there early to get a good spot. How about if I prepare pancakes for us in the morning around eight?"

"You sure? I wouldn't want you to go to any trouble."

She waved off his words. "No problem. I told you I enjoy cooking."

After they finished dinner, he told her he needed to leave to read some reports for work, which wasn't a lie. She walked him to the door. He leaned down to kiss her, intending for it to be a light touch of their lips.

But the moment his mouth touched hers and she released a breathless sigh, it seemed the most natural thing to slide his tongue inside her mouth and deepen the kiss. Wrapping his arms around her waist, he pulled her tight against him and knew the exact moment the kiss had changed to something more.

It was no longer a *goodbye and I'll see you later* kiss. Instead it was one of those *I need to have you before I go* kind. And Swan seemed to be reciprocating those feelings as she returned the kiss with equal fervor.

The next thing Flipper knew, he was sweeping her off her feet and moving quickly toward her bedroom. When he placed her on the bed, they began stripping off their clothes.

For him, she'd become an itch he couldn't scratch and a craving that wouldn't go away. There was something about making love to her that made every part of his body ache with need. She had imprinted herself on his soul and in every bone in his body and there was nothing he could do about it but savor what they had for as long as he could.

When she was completely naked, his pulse kicked up a notch and his breathing was forced from his lungs when he looked at her. She was beautiful and perfectly made.

He pulled a condom from his wallet in the shorts she'd helped him remove and toss aside. Knowing she was watching his every move, he rolled it over his aroused manhood.

"I want to do that for you the next time."

He looked at Swan. "All right." So she was letting him know she intended there to be a next time for them. He was glad because he wanted a next time, too.

There was a big chance when she found out the truth about why he was here on the island that she wouldn't want to have anything to do with him again. But he forced the thought from his mind.

"You don't have all evening, you know," she teased.

She was right, he didn't and it was a good thing she didn't know why. He moved toward her. "Impatient?"

She smiled up at him. "Yes, you could say that."

"In that case, I can help you with that problem." He leaned in. "I've got to taste you again," was all he said just seconds before his mouth came down on hers.

Swan automatically lifted her arms around his neck the moment his lips touched hers.

Capturing her tongue, David drew it into his mouth. Blood rushed fast and furious to Swan's head, making her feel both light-headed and dazed as his tongue began mating with hers. His technique was rousing her passion to a level that electrified every part of her. Insistent need rushed up her spine, spinning her senses and mesmerizing her with his delectable taste.

He suddenly broke off the kiss and they both panted furiously, drawing deep gulps of air into their lungs.

She rested her head against his chest and inhaled his scent as she continued to catch her breath. She knew she was losing herself to passion again when she felt the hardness of his erection brushing against her thigh, energizing the area between her legs.

Then she heard him whispering erotic details of what he wanted to do to her. His words spread fire through her body and when he gently cupped the area between her legs, she moaned.

"You're torturing me, David," she said, before twisting to push him down on his back so she could straddle him. Before he could react, she lowered her head between his masculine thighs and eased his erection into her mouth.

"Ah, Swan," he growled huskily, gripping her hair. She was fully aware of him expanding and felt a sense of triumph in her ability to get him even more aroused than he already was. The feel of his hands locked in her hair sparked even more passion within her and motivated her to use her mouth in ways she'd never done before.

"Swan!"

She felt his thighs flex beneath her hands before he bucked forward. She wasn't prepared when he quickly switched their positions so that she was the one on her back. The blue eyes staring down at her flared with a passion that sent tremors through her.

Before she could whisper his name, he slid inside her. He kept going deeper and deeper, stretching her in ways she didn't know she could be spread, inch by inch.

"Wrap your legs around me, baby," he whispered in a throaty voice.

When she did as he asked, he began thrusting hard. It was as if his total concentration was on her, intent on giving her pleasure. She felt every inch of him as he rode her hard, not letting up.

"David!"

She screamed his name as he continued to make

love to her, throwing her into a euphoric state that seemed endless. He was using her legs to keep their bodies locked while relentlessly pounding into her. Her world was spinning and she couldn't control the need to moan, moan and moan some more.

She was unable to hold anything back when her body erupted into an orgasm so powerful it propelled her toward utter completeness. She screamed his name once again as a deep feeling of ecstasy ripped through her entire body.

Flipper eased off Swan to lie beside her. Pulling her into his arms, his nostrils flared as he inhaled the scent of sex. The scent of woman, this woman. A woman he still desired even now.

He was not new to lust. Been there, done that and he figured he would be doing it some more. A lot more. With Swan lying in in his arms, snuggled close to him, close to his heart, he knew something had changed between them.

Bottom line, Swan Jamison was not only intoxicating, she was addictive.

"I don't think I'll be able to move again, David."

A smile touched the corners of his lips. He definitely knew how she felt, but he knew he had to move. He had somewhere to be tonight and as sexually drained as he was, he intended to be there.

"Then don't move. Just lie there. I'll let myself out," he said, reluctant to go, although he knew he must.

"You sure?" she asked in a lethargic voice.

"Positive. I'll be back in the morning for the parade and then we have a date on Friday."

"Yes. I'm going to need it. I'll be working late Wednesday doing inventory. I probably won't leave work until around ten."

"With your worker's help?"

"No. The cruise ship comes in Wednesday."

He released her to ease out of bed and put on his clothes. "What does a cruise ship have to do with anything?" He could feel her gaze on his body. He couldn't disguise the impact of knowing she was watching him. He was getting aroused all over again.

"Jamila dates a guy who works on the cruise ship and they only see each other whenever the ship comes to port. She always requests the day off to spend with him. I guess they made up."

He had planned to check out Jamila's house when he'd assumed she would be at work. Good thing he now knew otherwise.

"Made up?" he asked, pulling his shirt over his head.

"Yes. I got the impression they weren't on good terms last week. Not sure what happened but it's all good now since they've apparently kissed and made up."

He nodded. "How long have they been to-gether?"

"About six months now."

Flipper didn't say anything as he continued dressing. There hadn't been any mention of a boyfriend for Jamila Fairchild in the report he'd read. Another discrepancy. There were too many inconsistencies for his liking and he was deter-mined to find out why. One thing was certain, he didn't like the idea of Swan being at her shop alone late at night.

He moved back to the bed, leaned down and brushed a kiss across her lips. "I'll see you in the morning."

"Looking forward to it."

He smiled down at her and then turned and left.

Later that night, Flipper, dressed all in black, moved in the shadows, careful to avoid street-lights and security cameras. He had scoped out the area and was familiar with where the cam-eras were located. More than once, he'd had to dart behind a shrub when people were out for a late-night stroll.

He reached the area where Swan's shop was lo-cated and when he heard voices, he darted behind a building to hide in the shadows.

Two men stood not far away. One of them was Rafe. Neither of the men saw Flipper. The other guy was a little taller and appeared to be a for-eigner. Their conversation sounded like an ar-gument and was in a language Flipper wasn't familiar with and he spoke four. Most SEALs spoke at least that many, except for Coop, who had mastered seven.

When the men lapsed into English, they lowered their voices and could barely be heard. Flipper did make out the words *ink* and *roses*. Was someone getting a tattoo of roses painted on their body? If so, did it mean anything?

Flipper was glad when the men finally moved on. More than ever, he was determined to check out the tattoo parlor. He waited a half hour to make sure the men didn't return. When he was certain they had gone, he went to work bypassing the security alarms and cameras.

Using a sort of skeleton key, he opened the back door and walked inside the tattoo parlor. Using night goggles, he glanced around.

The place looked like a typical tattoo parlor. He should know since he and his brothers had frequented a number of them. He was proud of the images on his body. Luckily, Swan hadn't asked him about them. He was glad because the last thing he wanted to do was lie about why he was into dolphins.

Pulling off the camera attached to his utility belt, he replaced the night goggles with a high-tech camera, which was his own creation. This particular piece of equipment detected objects underground and under water. Looking through the lens, he scanned the room. It wasn't long before the camera light began blinking.

He moved toward the area and aimed the camera lower, toward the floor, and the blinking increased. Evidently something was buried beneath the wooden floor, a portion covered by a rug. The architectural report he'd been given of Swan's shop had not exposed any secret rooms or closets.

Putting the camera aside, he moved the rug and felt around to find a latch. He opened the trapdoor to find a small compartment beneath the floor. He saw more containers of ink. Why? There was a supply case full of ink on the opposite side of the room. Why was this ink hidden?

The first thing he noticed was the difference in the labeling. Was there something different about this particular ink? There was only one way to find out, he thought, taking one out of the cubby. He would overnight one of the containers to Nick instead of naval intelligence.

At this stage of the game, he wasn't taking any chances about who could be trusted.

Nine

Swan had just finished the last of her inventory when she heard the knock on her shop's door. Crossing the room, she peeped through the blinds to see who it was. A smile touched her lips as she unlocked the door. "David, I didn't think I'd see you until Friday."

He glanced around her empty shop before looking back at her. "I finished work early and remembered you saying you were working late tonight doing inventory. I wanted to make sure you got home okay."

That was really nice of him. "You didn't have

to do that." But she was glad he had. They had spent Monday together celebrating Memorial Day. He had arrived at her place for breakfast and then they'd walked to where the start of the parade would take place.

After the parade, they'd gone to the island festival marketplace where various vendors had lined the streets with booths and a huge Ferris wheel. They had taken one of the boat rides around the islands and had ended up eating lunch on Key Largo.

She had thought about him a lot since Monday, remembering in explicit detail how he'd made love to her before leaving.

"I know you said Jamila would be off today," David said. "What about your tattoo guy? Is the parlor closed on Wednesdays as well?"

"Yes, but Rafe dropped by earlier. He was expecting a shipment of more ink to come in today but it didn't. He wasn't happy about that."

"He wasn't?"

"No. He said there was a particular shade of blue he was expecting."

Flipper nodded and checked his watch. "Ready to go?"

"Yes, I just need to grab my purse from my office." She was about to turn to get it when there was another knock at the door.

"Expecting anyone?" David asked her.

"No. I'll see who it is."

She walked to the door and David went with her. After glancing out of the blinds, she turned back to David and smiled. "It's Jamila and Horacio."

She unlocked the door. "Jamila, hi."

"Hey, Swan. Horacio and I were in the neighborhood and I remembered you would be here late. I thought we'd drop by to say hello."

Swan smiled at the man with Jamila. "Horacio, it's good seeing you again."

"Same here, Swan," he said in a heavy accent that Swan always loved hearing.

"And this is my friend David Holloway. David, you already know Jamila. This is her friend Horacio Jacinto," Swan said, making introductions.

The two men shook hands. Swan wondered

if she'd imagined it but she thought David had tensed up when he'd seen Jamila and Horacio. "Nice meeting you, Horacio," David said. "I can't place your accent. Where are you from?"

"Portugal."

"Nice country," David said.

"Thanks."

"I hope you'll leave before it gets too late, Swan," Jamila was saying.

"I will. David came to make sure I got home okay." Usually whenever she worked late, either doing inventory or making her jewelry, she would catch a cab home even though she lived only a few blocks away. But since David was here, she would suggest they walk. It was a nice night and she would love to spend more time with him.

"We'll see you guys later," Jamila said. "We had dinner at Marty's Diner and now we're going to Summer Moon for drinks and live music."

"Okay. Enjoy. And I hope to see you again the next time the ship ports, Horacio," Swan said.

Horacio smiled. "I hope to see you as well."

After they left, Swan went to her office to get

her purse. She returned and noticed David was standing in the same spot where she'd left him, staring at the door. "Are you all right?"

He turned to her. "Yes, it's just that Horacio looks familiar and I was trying to remember when I might've seen him. Maybe I've run into him before, here on the island."

She nodded. "That's possible. He's a chef on the Century Cruise Line that docks here once a week. Whenever it does, he comes ashore and meets up with Jamila. I think I mentioned that to you."

"You did, but I could have sworn I saw him a few nights ago. Sunday. After leaving your place."

Swan shook her head. "It wasn't him. The ship didn't arrive in our port until today. But you know what they say about everybody having a twin."

He chuckled. "You're probably right, but I'm sure you don't have one. I'm convinced there's not another woman anywhere who is as beautiful as you."

Swan knew better than to let such compliments go to her head, but she couldn't help the smile that spread across her lips. "You, David Holloway, can make a girl's head swell if she's inclined to believe whatever you say."

"I hope you do believe it because I spoke the truth." He took her hand in his as they headed for the door.

Flipper pulled out his phone the minute he walked into his hotel room later that night. He'd felt it vibrate in his pocket when he was walking Swan home but figured it would be a call he needed to take in private.

Swan had invited him inside but he'd declined, telling her he had a ton of paperwork waiting on him back at his hotel. That wasn't a lie. He'd begun rereading all those naval intelligence reports to see if he could determine why those investigators had failed to do their job and instead intentionally went after Swan as a scapegoat.

He checked his phone and saw Nick had called and Flipper quickly returned the call. "What do you have for me?"

"More than you counted on. All I can say is

whoever handled that investigation did a botched-up job."

Or they did the job they'd been expected to do, Flipper thought. "I guess there's a reason you feel that way."

"Yes. That ink you sent to be analyzed isn't what it's supposed to be."

"It's not ink?"

"Yes, it's ink, but coded ink. When applied to the skin as a tattoo, it can be decoded by a special light. It's my guess that's how the classified information is leaving Swan Jamison's shop—with people's tattoos and not with any of her jewelry. Guess where the ink is being shipped from."

"Swan mentioned from some place in California."

"Yes, that's right and the distribution company is a few miles from the naval base in San Diego. That means someone on the base must be passing classified information that's being shipped in the ink."

Flipper frowned. "And because Rafe Duggers

is conveniently including Swan's stones with each shipment, it makes sense for her to be suspect."

"Right," Nick agreed. "Someone is setting her up real good, Flipper. They are definitely making her the fall guy."

Flipper wondered who in naval intelligence had targeted Swan and why. "I have another piece of the puzzle I need you to check out."

"What?"

"The guy who was with Rafe Duggers two nights ago. The one I told you he was arguing with. I saw him today."

"You did?"

"Yes. He came into the shop when Swan was closing up. His name is Horacio Jacinto and he's Jamila Fairchild's boyfriend."

"That's interesting. I'll find out what I can about him," Nick said. "I wonder if Ms. Fairchild knows what's going on or if she's being used as a pawn."

"I don't know, but I'm going to make sure I keep an eye on all of them."

"Be careful, Flipper."

"I will."

A few hours later, after taking a shower, Flipper was sitting at the desk in his hotel room suite when his cell phone went off. Recognizing the ringtone, he clicked on and said, "What's going on, Coop?"

"You tell us."

Us meant Bane, Viper and Mac were also on the phone. "I guess Nick called you guys."

"Yes, he called us earlier today," Bane said. "What's going on with Swan Jamison sounds pretty damn serious. Don't you think it's time to call the CO?"

Flipper ran a hand down his face. He glanced at the clock on the wall. It was close to three in the morning. "If Nick told you everything, then you know it's an inside job at the base. There's a traitor somewhere and until I know who I can trust, then—"

"You know as well as we do that you can trust our CO, Flipper," Viper said. "Once you tell Shields what you've found out, if he suspects Martin or Levart of any wrongdoing, he will know what to do."

"Yes, however, the three of them share a close friendship. What if the CO is blinded due to loyalty?"

"We're talking about our commanding officer, Flipper. Shields would turn his own mother in if he thought she was betraying our country. You know that."

Yes, he knew it. But still… "I don't know if Martin or Levart is really involved. Like Shields, they are Swan's godfathers and I would hate to think they are shady. I just know it's an inside job and right now I'm suspicious of just about everybody."

"We figured you would be, so open the damn door," Mac said.

Flipper frowned. "What?"

"We said open the door," Coop said, knocking.

Flipper heard the knock, clicked off his phone, quickly went to the door and snatched it open. There stood his four best friends.

"What are you guys doing here?"

"What does it look like?" Mac asked as the four moved passed Flipper to enter the hotel room.

"We figured ten pairs of eyes were better than two," Bane said, glancing around. "Besides, we need to keep you objective."

"But what about your families? Viper, your wife is having a baby!"

Viper chuckled. "And I plan to be there when she does. According to Layla's doctor, we still have a couple of months, so I'm good."

"And our families are good, too," Coop said. "They know we look out for each other and they agreed we should be here for you."

"Teri is glad I'm gone," Mac said, grumbling. "Maybe when I go back, she'll have a new attitude."

"Or maybe you'll have one," Bane said, frowning at Mac.

"Whatever," Mac said, picking up the hotel's restaurant menu book. "Is it too late for room service?"

Flipper closed the door and drew in a deep breath as he watched the men gather around the table, already rolling up their sleeves, ready to help him figure things out. They worked together as a team and he would admit that whenever they did so, good things happened.

"There's something all of you should know," he said, getting their attention.

They glanced over at him. "What? No room service at this hour?" Mac asked in a serious tone.

"That, too."

"What's the other thing we should know, Flipper?" Viper asked, sitting back in the chair he'd claimed as soon as he came in.

Flipper leaned against the closed door. "Investigating Swan Jamison is no longer just an assignment for me. It's become personal."

The men nodded. "And you think we don't know that, Flipper?" Coop asked in a steely tone. "That's why we're here. Someone is trying to frame your woman and we're going to help you find out who and why. But first things first. You know what you have to do, right?"

Flipper stared at the four men. Yes, he knew. Instead of answering Coop, he picked up his cell phone from the table and placed a call to his CO.

Ten

As far as Swan was concerned, Friday hadn't arrived fast enough. With every passing hour, she would glance at her shop's door expecting to see David walk in. One would think his surprise visit Wednesday would have sufficed. Unfortunately, it hadn't.

She'd had two days to think about how irrational her thoughts about David were becoming. He didn't come across as a forever sort of guy and she wasn't looking for a forever kind of relationship, so what was up with this urgency to see him?

The only reason she could give herself was that

she'd been alone and without a man's attention for so long that now that she had it, she was in greedy mode, lapping it up like a desperate woman. And she had never done the desperate thing before.

The door chimed and she looked up to see that it was Rafe who walked in. Lately she'd noticed him using the front door a lot more, instead of the back door to his parlor. They had decided at the beginning of his lease that the entrance to her shop was off-limits so his customers wouldn't trounce back and forth through her shop on the days Rafe worked late.

"Did your box of ink finally arrive?"

He stopped and looked over at her. "Why would you be asking about my ink?"

Now that, she thought, was a silly question. Did the man have a short memory? "Because you came by Wednesday looking for the shipment and left in a tiff when it hadn't arrived."

"I wasn't in a tiff and yes, I did get my box of ink."

Yes, he had been in a tiff, but if he wouldn't

acknowledge it, then she would leave it alone. "Good. I'm glad you got it."

She watched him walk off toward his parlor. He hadn't been in a good mood lately. But then, maybe she'd been in such an extremely good mood that she had a distorted view. In fact, come to think of it, it was pretty normal for him to be moody.

Moments later, while she worked with a customer, Swan watched as Rafe walked back through her shop and toward the front door. She decided if he did that again she would remind him of their agreement about which door he should use whenever he went in or out of his tattoo parlor.

After her customer left, she glanced at her watch. Her shop would be closing in a couple of minutes. David usually arrived early. It would be understandable if he'd gotten detained, but she hoped he hadn't been. She was so anxious to see him.

The thought of how much she was looking forward to being with him should bother her, but for some reason it didn't. Like she'd told Candy, Swan wasn't expecting anything from her relationship with David. There had been no promises made, so none would be broken. The only thing she was expecting was exactly what she was getting—a good time. He was excellent company and great in bed.

It had been almost three years since William, and during that time, although she'd dated, she hadn't allowed herself to get serious over a man. Instead she had concentrated on opening her shop and making it a success.

She had put her mind, heart and soul into Swan's. Especially her heart, deciding that if she put it into her business, she wouldn't run the risk of placing it elsewhere. Now it seemed there might be a risk after all and that risk had a name. David Holloway.

A part of her wanted to protect herself from another possible heartbreak by calling David and canceling any plans for tonight and then to stop sharing any time with him after that. He had given her his number so she could reach him. She could certainly come up with a plausible excuse. But did she really want to do that?

No, she didn't.

David would be her test. If she could handle a casual affair with him, then she would ace the test with flying colors.

The door chimed and she glanced up and there he was. She watched him lock her door and put the Closed sign in place before pulling down the blinds. Then he slowly sauntered toward her wearing a pair of khaki pants and an open white shirt and holding her within the scope of those laser-blue eyes. There was his too-sexy walk and a smile that made her heart beat rapidly.

Suddenly seeing him, when she'd been thinking of him all day, took complete control of her senses. Without much effort, the man had turned the sensuality up more than a notch. He had his own barometer of hotness.

Finally moving her feet, she strolled across the floor to meet him halfway and walked straight into his arms. The moment he pressed his body to hers, she reached up and looped her arms around his neck. He responded by wrapping his arms around her waist, drawing her even closer so she fit against him.

"I missed you, Swan."

She shouldn't let his words affect her, but they did—to the point where she was having difficulty replying.

"I missed you, too."

And she had, although they'd seen each other Wednesday. Even when she'd tried to convince herself that missing him to such a degree meant nothing. Now, as she stood wrapped in his arms, with her body pressed tight against his, hip to hip and thigh to thigh, she knew it meant everything.

"That's good to know, sweetheart," he said in a throaty voice.

Sweetheart? The endearment left her defenseless. She was trying to summon all her senses to regroup. And it wasn't helping matters that his arousal was cradled in the apex of her thighs. Good Lord, he felt so good there.

"Ready?" she found the voice to ask him.

His gaze studied her face as if he was seeing

her for the first time. As if he was trying to record her features to memory. And then a mischievous smile touched his lips. "I'm ready for whatever you have in mind, Swan."

Shivers of desire skittered down her spine and Swan wished his words hadn't given her ideas, but they had. Ideas that were so bold, brazen and shameless she felt her cheeks staining just thinking about them. But at that moment, she didn't care. She could and would admit to wanting him.

She should wait until later to act on her desires. That would be the safe thing to do. But she knew she would be tortured during dinner whenever she looked at him. The way his mouth moved when he ate, or the way his hands—those hands that could turn her on just by looking at them—gripped his beer bottle. There were so many things about David Holloway that would do her in if she were to wait until later.

"You sure about that, David?"

"Positive. Do you want me to prove it?"

Did she? Yes, she did. "Where?"

"I will prove it anywhere you want. Right here

in the middle of the floor if you like," he said. "But I suggest your office."

Flipper could tell by the way she was looking at him that she was giving his offer serious thought. He had no problems tilting the scale in his favor and he decided to do so. Lowering his head, he kissed her, trying to be gentle and finding gentleness hard to achieve. Especially when her taste made him greedy for more.

He knew she'd ceased thinking when she responded to his kiss by sinking her body farther into his embrace and tightening her arms around his neck.

Some things, he decided then and there, were just too mind-blowingly good, and kissing Swan was one of them. What they'd shared these last few days was a dimension of pleasure he hadn't felt in a long time—or maybe ever—while devouring a woman's mouth. And when his hands shifted from around her waist to cup her backside, he groaned at the feel of her body pressed tightly against his erection.

When he finally broke off the kiss, he buried his face in the curve of her neck and drew in a deep breath. This woman was almost too much. She looked good, tasted good and as he drew in another deep breath, he concluded that she smelled good, too.

"You want to come with me, Mr. Holloway?" she asked, stepping out of his arms.

"Yes." The answer was quick off his lips.

She took his hand. "Then follow me."

He had no problem following her and the minute he crossed the threshold into her office, he recalled the last time he'd been in here. Namely, when they'd shared a kiss that had nearly brought him to his knees.

"It appears dinner will have to wait."

He glanced over at her. She had stepped out of her sandals. After locking the office door, he leaned against it and watched her undress. She was wearing a burnt-orange sundress with spaghetti straps. It looked good on her and the color of the dress seemed to highlight her hair and skin tone.

He had gotten little sleep since his friends had arrived in the Keys. But then they hadn't come here to rest. They had left their families to come here and help him solve a sinister plan of espionage against the country they loved.

And to protect the woman *he* loved.

He suddenly swallowed deep when that last thought passed through his mind. As he watched Swan remove her panties, he knew without a doubt that he had fallen in love with her. He wouldn't try to figure out how it happened but just accept that it had. Now more than ever he was determined to make sure whoever was trying to screw her over didn't succeed.

"Are you going to just stand there?" she asked, standing before him completely naked.

"No, that's not my intention at all," he said, moving away from the door to stand a few feet from her in what he considered his safe zone. If he got any closer, he would be tempted to take her with his clothes on. He removed his shirt and eased both his khakis and briefs down his legs at the same time. Quick and easy.

"I love your dolphins," she said. "I meant to ask you about them a number of other times, but always got sidetracked. So I'm asking you now. Any reason you chose dolphins?"

He decided to be as truthful with her as he could. One day he would have to explain to her why he'd lied about so many things. "Like the dolphins, I love being in the water. But this isn't just any dolphin."

"It's not?"

"No. This dolphin's name is Flipper. Surely you've heard of him."

"Not as much as I know Willy from *Free Willy*."

He chuckled as he moved toward her. "Willy was a whale. Flipper was a dolphin. That's what my friends call me. Flipper."

"Flipper?"

"Yes. Like I said, I love being in the water."

"You don't look like a Flipper."

He came to a stop in front of her. "Don't tell that to my family and friends. They wouldn't agree with you."

She reached out and touched the tattoo of the

dolphin on his arm. Her fingers felt like fire as she traced along the design with her fingertips. "Beautiful. Not just your tattoos but all of you, David."

"Thanks." And in one smooth sweep, he picked her up and sat her on the desk, spreading her legs in the process.

"Did I tell you how much I missed you?" he asked, running his hands over her arms.

"Yes. Just a few moments ago when you arrived here and I told you I missed you, too. You also told me that you missed me when you walked me home Wednesday night and I invited you to stay."

Flipper heard the disappointment in her voice. If only she knew how much he'd wanted to stay. But once he'd found out Jamila would be out for a while with Horacio, he needed that time to check out her place. "I couldn't, but I intend to make it up to you when we have more time."

He was letting her know this little quickie didn't count. He had something planned for her when all this was over and he could sit her down and tell her everything.

"Not here and not now? What do you call this?" she asked when he reached up and cupped her breasts in his hands, marveling at just how beautiful they were.

"This is an I-can't-wait-until-later quickie."

"Interesting."

Shifting his gaze from her breasts to her eyes, he said, "Let me show you, Swan Jamison, just how interesting it can be." He leaned forward and kissed her while placing the head of his erection against her wet opening. The contact sent heat spiraling through him.

While his tongue mated greedily with hers, he entered her in one hard stroke. Pulling his mouth from hers, he let out a guttural moan when her muscles clamped down on his throbbing erection. That made him push harder and sink deeper.

And when she moaned his name, he knew she could feel the fire of passion spreading between them as much as he could.

Swan wrapped her legs completely around Flipper, loving the feel of him moving inside her. He was giving her body one heck of a workout on her desk. She could feel the heat in his eyes as he stared at her.

He used his hands to lift her hips off the desk's surface for a deeper penetration. When his erection hit a certain part of her, she gasped and arched her back.

"David…"

She whispered his name when she felt him going deeper and deeper. The intensity of their joining sent emotions skyrocketing through her.

She needed this. She wanted this. Like him, she needed it now, not later. This was more than interesting. This was a hot, frenzied, torrid mating. More than a quickie. David was thorough, meticulously so, and not to be rushed. It was as if he intended to savor every stroke.

Suddenly, she felt herself falling. Not off the desk but out of reality when an orgasm rammed through her at the same time as he shuddered with the force of his own release.

They stared at each other, realizing something

at the same time. Wanting to make sure he didn't stop, she whispered, "Pill."

It seemed that single word triggered another orgasm and she felt him flooding her insides again while his deep, guttural groan filled the room. His release sparked another within her. His name was torn from her lips when her body shattered in earth-shaking and mind-blowing ecstasy.

As the daze from Swan's orgasmic state receded, she felt David slowly withdraw from inside her. That's when she forced her eyes open to stare at him and accepted the hand he extended to help her off the desk. Once on her feet, she wrapped her arms around his waist, feeling weak in the knees.

"It's okay, baby, I got you. I won't let you fall," he whispered close to her ear as he leaned down.

Too late, she thought. She'd already fallen. Head over heels in love with him. The very thought suddenly sent her mind spinning.

Hadn't she just given herself a good talking to moments before he'd arrived? Told herself he was someone she could enjoy, both in and out of bed and nothing more? That he was someone she knew better than to give her heart to because she hadn't wanted to take the risk?

What on earth had happened?

She knew the answer as she moved closer into the comfort of his warm naked body. David Holloway had happened. As much as she hadn't meant to fall in love with him, she had.

It didn't matter that she had known him less than three weeks. Somehow he had come into her world and turned it upside down, whether that had been his intent or not. When his work on the island was finished, he would move on and not look back. But still, knowing that he would leave hadn't stopped him from winning her heart.

"Ready?"

She lifted her head and look up at him. "You know, David, that lone question will get us in trouble."

He held her gaze for a long moment and then caressed the side of her face. "Or take us to places we really want to go and inspire us to do things that we really want to do."

Then he lowered his mouth to hers and kissed her.

Eleven

"Great work finding out about that ink, Lieutenant Holloway. I knew there was no way Swan would have betrayed her country."

"Yes, sir. Those are my thoughts as well," Flipper said. He had placed his CO on speakerphone so his SEAL teammates could listen to the call. "There's no doubt in my mind the persons naval intelligence should be concentrating on are Rafe Duggers and Horacio Jacinto."

"I agree. I met with Admiral Martin and Director Levart this morning and they concur there's a mole within the organization."

"By meeting with them, sir, does that mean you feel certain they can be totally trusted as well?" Flipper felt he had to ask.

"Yes, Lieutenant Holloway. I do. I know that because of what you discovered and what went down with Lieutenant Westmoreland a few years ago involving those moles at Homeland Security, you're not sure who you can trust. I understand that. However, I assure you that you can trust the three of us to protect Swan with our lives if we have to. We knew she was innocent, which was why we sent you there to prove we were right. You have. Now it's up to us to find out who's behind this and bring them to justice."

"And in the meantime?"

"In the meantime, Lieutenant, you are free to consider this assignment completed. Go home to Texas and enjoy the remainder of your leave."

There was no way he could consider this assignment completed, although under normal circumstances it would be once the CO said so. "I think I'll hang around Key West for a while."

"Why?" Commanding Officer Shields asked.

"Do you think Swan's life might be in immediate danger?"

"As long as Duggers and Jacinta don't know they're suspected of anything, then no. However..."

"However what, Lieutenant Holloway?"

Flipper had no problem being truthful to his CO. "However, Swan has come to mean a lot to me, sir."

"Oh, I see."

Flipper figured since his CO knew him so well, he did see. "In that case, Lieutenant Holloway, how you choose to spend the rest of your leave is your decision. But keep in mind, since this is an ongoing investigation, you cannot tell Swan anything, including your reason for being in the Keys in the first place. That in itself will place you in what might be perceived by her as a dishonorable situation."

"I'm aware of that, sir, but I refuse to leave her until I have to. How long do you think it will take to wrap up the investigation?"

"Not sure. We will not only be investigating

the original investigators but we'll have to restart the entire case, making Duggers and Jacinta the primary suspects. If you remain in the Keys and notice anything I need to know, don't hesitate to bring it to my attention."

In other words, Commanding Officer Shields was pretty much giving Flipper the green light to do his own thing, unofficially. "Yes, sir."

When Flipper clicked off the phone, he glanced up at his friends. "So what do you guys think?"

"Personally, I think you're doing the right thing not leaving here until you're certain Miss Jamison's life is not in any danger," Bane said.

"And since we don't plan to leave until you do, it's time we figure out just who is behind this," Coop added.

"I agree with all the above," Viper tacked on.

They all looked at Mac, who rubbed his chin as if contemplating something. Then he said, "Someone needs to play devil's advocate, so I guess it has to be me."

"No surprise there," Bane said.

Mac shot Bane a glare and then glanced back

at Flipper. "Think about what the CO said. You can't tell Miss Jamison anything. Once she finds out the truth, that she was nothing more than an assignment to you, she's not going to like it, no matter how noble or honorable your intentions might have been."

Flipper drew in a deep breath. He knew Mac's words to be true. Although Swan had yet to tell him anything about her affair with William Connors, it had been in the report. The man had betrayed her and there was a chance she would probably see Flipper as doing the same. "So, Mr. Know-It-All, what do you suggest I do?" he asked.

"Start drawing a line in your relationship and don't cross it. In other words, stop seducing her," Mac said.

Too late for that, Flipper thought. All he had to do was remember what they'd done yesterday in Swan's office and again when he'd taken her home after dinner. Especially when he'd sat in one of her kitchen chairs and she'd straddled his body. The memories of what had started out in that chair and ended up in her bedroom made him feel hot. He hadn't left her place until dawn this morning. There was no way he could put a freeze on his relationship with Swan like Mac was suggesting.

"That's not an option, Mac. I'm going to do what I have to do now and worry about the consequences later."

"What's this about you having a boyfriend? I can't leave you alone for one minute."

Swan smiled when she glanced up at Rosie McCall, one of her frequent customers. Rosie, an older woman in her midforties who'd been away for the past three months visiting her family in Nevada, had returned to the Keys just yesterday. "I see Jamila has been talking again."

"Doesn't matter. So tell me, who is he?"

Swan closed the jewelry case. "First of all, he's not my boyfriend. He's just someone I'm seeing while he's here on the island working, which won't be much longer."

"Um, short meaningless flings are the best kind. What's his name?"

"David. David Holloway."

"Where he is from?"

"Texas."

"You said he's here working. What does he do for a living?"

"Whoa, time-out," Swan said, using her hand for the signal. "You don't need to know all that. David's a nice guy and that's all you really need to know."

She knew how Rosie liked to play matchmaker. She'd been the one who'd introduced Jamila to Horacio. Rosie had met him at one of the nightclubs and thought he was cute, too young for her but just the right age for Swan or Jamila. Swan hadn't been interested in a blind date but Jamila had. Horacio and Jamila met, hit it off and had been an item ever since.

"You can't blame me for being curious, Swan. You seldom date."

"My choice, remember? Besides, you do it enough for the both of us." And that was the truth. After her second divorce, Rosie had made it known she would never marry again but intended to date any man who asked her out as long as they were the right age. Not too old and not too young.

Rosie smiled. "Yes, I do, don't I? But that doesn't mean you shouldn't go out and have fun every once in a while. There's more to life than this shop, Swan. I hope you're finally finding that out."

"Whatever." Swan had heard it before and all from Rosie. She liked the older woman and thought she was a fun person who had a zeal for life. There was never a dull moment around her.

At that moment, the shop's door chimed and Swan knew without looking in that direction that David had walked in. She also knew when he saw her with a customer that he would wait until she finished before approaching her.

Rosie leaned in. "Looks like you have a customer. Let's hope he buys something since he came in a minute before closing."

Swan inwardly smiled. "We can only hope, right?"

"But then he's such a cutie. Look at him."

Swan didn't have to look at David to know what a cutie he was, but she did so anyway. He was browsing around the store wearing a pair of shorts and a sleeveless T-shirt with flip-flops on his feet. He looked laid-back and sexy as sin. "You're right, he is a cutie."

"I love those tattoos on his upper arms. Nice."

"Yes, they are." She knew Rosie was into tattoos and was one of Rafe's frequent customers. The woman had them everywhere, visible and non-visible.

"You need to go wait on him. See what he wants. If he's not sure, offer him a few things."

Swan smiled. Little did Rosie know, but she intended to offer David a lot. "I will. Come on, I'll walk you to the door. I'm officially closed now," Swan said, coming from around the counter.

"You honestly want me to leave you here with him?" Rosie whispered. "For all you know he's not safe."

Swan chuckled and decided it was time for her to come clean. "He's safe, Rosie. That's David and he's here to walk me home. I'll introduce you on your way out the door."

"You mean that gorgeous hunk is your guy?"

Swan glanced over at David again. He was definitely a gorgeous hunk but she couldn't claim him as her guy. "Yes, he's the guy I've been seeing a lot of lately."

"Smart girl."

David glanced up when they approached and gave her a huge smile. "Hi," he greeted.

"Hi, David. I'd like you to meet Rosie McCall. A friend who has been away for the past few months and just returned back to the island. Rosie, this is David Holloway."

David extended his hand. "Nice meeting you, Rosie."

"Same here, David. I like your tattoos."

"Thanks and I like yours," he responded.

"Thanks. Well, I'll be going. I hope you guys enjoy yourselves."

"We will," Swan said, smiling up at David. "I'll be back after seeing Rosie out," she told him.

He nodded. "Nice meeting you, Rosie."

"Same here."

Swan returned to David a few moments later, after putting up the Closed sign, locking the door and pulling down the shades. She turned and studied him as he stood across the room, looking so amazingly sexy. She felt a lump in her throat. She loved everything about him, especially the muscles beneath his shirt, the masculine thighs and his tanned skin.

"Got more sun today, I see."

"Yes, I had to go out on the boat today."

"One day you're going to have to explain to me in detail just what your ocean duties entail."

"I will. But for now, come here. I missed you today."

She crossed the room to walk into his arms. "I missed you, too."

"That's good to know. Rosie seems like a nice person."

"She is."

"She has a lot of tattoos."

Swan chuckled. "Yes, she does. She's one of Rafe's best customers."

"Is that right?" David asked, still smiling. "He did an awesome job."

She checked her watch. "We can leave as soon as I grab my purse." They would be having dinner at Nathan Waterway and afterward would attend an art show. "I'll be back in a second."

Flipper watched Swan walk off toward her office while thinking of what she'd told him about Rosie McCall. He recalled what he'd overheard Rafe and Horacio arguing about that night behind this building. Ink and roses. Or had they said Rosie? Was she a part of the group? If she was, that meant she had an ulterior motive for befriending Swan.

Pulling his phone from his pocket he texted Nick. Check out Rosie McCall.

He received an immediate reply. Will do.

He then texted Bane. Excursion tonight.

The reply was quick. On it.

Most of today he and Viper had pretended to go fishing after Mac, who'd been tailing Rafe for the past two days, reported that Rafe had rented a boat and headed in the direction of another island close by. Today Flipper and Viper had also rented a boat, making sure they stayed a good distance behind Duggers.

The man had docked in Fleming Key. Bane and Cooper, who'd arrived ahead of them, picked up the tail on Rafe. It seemed the man had gone into a sports shop where he'd stayed for three hours.

Pretending to be two guys enjoying their time out on their boat, Flipper and Viper had waited at the pier and knew when Rafe had left the island to return to Key West. Mac had been there to pick up the tail and reported that the man had been carrying a package when he went inside his tattoo shop. A package Rafe had gotten from the sports shop, according to Bane and Coop.

"I'm ready."

He looked up and when Swan met his gaze, she quickly clarified, "I'm ready *for dinner*."

He placed his phone back into his pocket and smiled. "That's all?"

The smile she returned made his insides quiver in anticipation. "For now, Mr. Holloway."

Twelve

It was getting harder and harder to leave Swan's bed, Flipper thought as he and his teammates docked at Fleming Key close to two in the morning. But at least he'd left her sleeping with the most peaceful smile on her face.

Without waking her, he had brushed a kiss across her lips and whispered that he loved her, knowing she would remember neither. But he decided to tell her how he felt when he saw her later today. He couldn't hold it inside any longer. She deserved to know. He wanted her to know. And when all this was over and she knew the truth, he would do whatever he needed to do to win her forgiveness and her love.

He jumped when fingers snapped in his face. He glared at Mac, who glared back. "Stay focused. You can daydream later."

"I wasn't daydreaming," Flipper countered. He then realized he was the only one still in the boat. The others had already gotten out.

"Then night-dreaming. Call it what you want" was Mac's reply. "Just get out of the damn boat."

Flipper didn't have to wonder why Mac was in a rotten mood. Teri had texted him earlier in the day to say the new washer and dryer had been delivered. They were new appliances Mac hadn't known they were buying.

Moments later, dressed in all black military combat gear, the five of them circled around to the back of the sports shop Rafe had frequented lately. Being ever ready and not taking any chances, Glocks were strapped to their hips and high powered tasers to their thighs. Due to Viper's hypersensitive ears—known to pick up sound over long distances away—he would stay outside as

the lookout. Flipper, Bane, Cooper and Mac by-
passed security cameras to enter the building.

Once inside, they used Flipper's cameras and it
didn't take long to find a hidden room. Making
swift use of their time, they took pictures of everything. It was obvious this was the group's operation headquarters. More tattoo ink was stored
here along with several specific tattoo designs.
One design Flipper quickly recalled seeing on
the side of Rosie's neck.

Flipper scanned the room with his camera and
then opened several drawers in the huge desk and
took photos of the contents. When he came across
a photo in one of the drawers, he suddenly froze.
"Damn."

"What is it, Flipper?" Bane asked.

Instead of saying anything, he motioned his
head to the photograph he'd found. Mac, Bane
and Coop came around him to see it as well. They
looked back at him and Mac said, "We've been
royally screwed."

An uneasy feeling settled in the pit of Flipper's
stomach. "I need to get back to Swan as soon as
possible."

* * *

Swan was awakened by the knocking on her door. She glanced at the clock on her nightstand and wondered who on earth would be at her house at four in the morning. Was it David returning? She didn't recall when he'd left but knew it was the norm for him to leave her place around midnight to return to his hotel because of his work. Usually she would be awake when he left but tonight sexual exhaustion had gotten the best of her.

Pulling on her robe, she tied it around her waist as she headed for the door. Looking out the peephole, she saw it was Jamila and Horacio. What were they doing out so late and why were they at her place? She found it odd that Horacio was on the island when the cruise ship wasn't due back in port again until next week.

From the look on Jamila's face, it appeared she wasn't happy about something. In fact, from her reddened eyes, it appeared that she'd been crying. Swan wondered what on earth was wrong. Had something happened?

Suddenly filled with concern, she quickly

opened the door. The minute she did so, Jamila was shoved inside, nearly knocking Swan down.

"Hey, wait a minute. What's going on?" Swan asked, fighting to regain her balance.

"Shut the hell up and don't ask questions," Horacio said, quickly coming inside and closing the door behind him.

Swan frowned. "Horacio? What do you mean, I can't ask any questions?"

"Just do what you're told," he barked.

Swan glanced over at Jamila and saw the bruise on the side of her face. "Did he do this to you?" Swan demanded, getting enraged. At Jamila's nod, Swan then turned to Horacio. How could he have done this when he adored Jamila? "I want you to leave now."

"If I don't, what are you going to do? Call the police? Or call that SEAL you're sleeping with?"

Swan frown deepened. "I don't know what you're talking about. Now leave or I *will* call the police."

"You won't be doing anything other than what

I tell you to do. When I get the word, the two of you will be coming with me."

Swan placed her hands on her hips. "We're not going anywhere with you."

A cynical smile touched Horacio's lips as he pulled out a gun from his back pocket. "This says you will."

Swan stared at the gun, not believing Horacio had it pointed at both her and Jamila. She was about to say something when Horacio added, "I'm giving you five minutes to go into your bedroom and put on clothes. Bring me your phone first. I don't want you to get any crazy ideas."

Swan had no idea what was going on, but from the pleading look in Jamila's eyes, she knew it was best to do as she was told. She went and got her cell phone and handed it to him, but not before she noticed several missed calls from David. Why had he been trying to call her? Her mind was filled with so many questions.

"You got five minutes to get dressed. If you're not back in five minutes or try some kind of funny business, your cousin here will pay for it."

Cousin? Why did he refer to Jamila as her cousin? At what was obviously a confused look on her face, he said, "That's right. Secrets. There are plenty more where those came from, Swan, and you'll be finding out about them later. Now go."

Swan got dressed in less than five minutes. If she hadn't thought Horacio was serious about hurting Jamila, she would have escaped through her bedroom window. That bruise along the side of her friend's face indicated the man was serious.

Swan was walking out of her bedroom fully dressed when Horacio's phone rang. Instead of answering it, he said, "That's my signal that things are ready. We'll go out your back door to the beach. The boat is waiting."

"What boat?"

"Please don't ask him anything, Swan," Jamila pleaded, reaching out and grabbing her arm. "All of them are crazy."

Swan wondered just who were *all of them*. But she decided not to ask.

"Move!"

Following Horacio's orders, she and Jamila walked toward Swan's kitchen to go out the back door.

As soon as their boat docked, Flipper raced through the streets of Key West toward Swan's home with his teammates fast on his heels. He had tried reaching her on the phone but didn't get an answer. He immediately knew something was wrong because she kept her phone on the nightstand next to her bed and the ringing would have woken her up. He had tried several more times with no luck, which was why his heart was beating out of control and fear was gripping his insides, especially now that he knew who was involved.

They had contacted their CO and told him what they'd discovered. He was as shocked as they'd been and they knew Shields would be taking the necessary actions on his end. Flipper hadn't had to tell the man there would be hell to pay if anyone hurt one single hair on Swan's head.

When they reached her house, they found the door unlocked. Her cell phone had been tossed on a living room table and a quick search of her bedroom indicated she'd change clothes.

"Take a look at this, Flipper," Mac called out.

When he reached them in the kitchen, Mac pointed out the window. Flipper saw lights from a boat that was sitting idle in the ocean as if waiting to rendezvous with another vessel.

"I traced footprints in the sand that led to the water. A small watercraft probably took them out to that boat," Viper was saying. "There were three sets of shoe prints belonging to two women and a man. And they left around thirty minutes ago."

Flipper raced out Swan's back door and after putting on his night-vision eyewear, he stared out at the ocean.

"Intercept with our boat," he shouted over his shoulder to the others. Quickly dropping to the sand, he began removing his shoes, T-shirt and pants, leaving his body clad in a pair of swimming trunks.

"Don't try it, Flipper. The boat's too far out," Mac said. "It's too dangerous for anyone, even you."

Flipper glanced up at them while putting the waterproof military belt that contained combat gear around his waist. He then put a pair of specially designed water goggles over his eyes. "The woman I love is on that boat and I have no idea what they plan to do, so I have to try. Even if I die trying."

Without saying anything else, he raced toward the water and dived in.

Horacio had tied their hands before forcing them into a small boat, which carried them out into the ocean to a much bigger boat. Now they were sitting idle in the waves.

Swan wondered why. She glanced around and noticed that, other than the lights on the boat, there was only darkness. They were so far from land she couldn't see the lights from the homes where she lived anymore.

As if Horacio realized she was trying to figure

out what was happening, he said, "I'm waiting for the rest of the gang, then we'll decide what we will do with the two of you."

What he said didn't make much sense. "Will someone please tell me what's going on?" Swan asked, getting angrier by the minute. None of this made any sense.

"I'll let your cousin go first since Jamila has a lot of explaining to do," Horacio said, grinning.

Swan turned to Jamila, who was sitting on a bench beside her. "What is he talking about? Why does he keep referring to you as my cousin?"

At first Jamila didn't say anything. In fact, it seemed she was refusing to meet Swan's gaze, but then she finally met Swan's eyes and said, "Because we are cousins, Swan. My mother is your grandfather's youngest sister."

"My grandfather?"

Jamila nodded. "Yes, Lawrence Jamison is my uncle. I knew for years that Uncle Lawrence disowned your father but I didn't know why until I was much older. Then I thought the reason was downright stupid and told the family what

I thought. Everyone else in the family thought the same thing but were too afraid to stand up to Uncle Lawrence."

Swan didn't say anything. She was still trying to dissect the fact that she and Jamila were related. She'd known from her father that Lawrence had a sister and another brother. That was all she'd known.

"When I turned twenty-one and finished college, I decided to come find you. Uncle Lawrence didn't like it but I told him I didn't care. I'm one of the few who stands up to him. He said the family would disown me if I came here."

"Yet you came anyway," Swan said.

"Yes, I came anyway."

Swan glanced over at Horacio. He wasn't saying anything and didn't appear to be listening to what they were saying. Instead he stood at the bow of the ship looking through binoculars as if he was searching for someone. He'd said they were waiting for another boat with the gang and Swan couldn't help but wonder who the gang was.

She wanted to ask Jamila how much she knew

and why they were being held hostage but figured that although Horacio was pretending not to listen to their conversation, he probably was.

Swan glanced over at Jamila. "Why didn't you tell me who you were when you first came into my shop that day? Why did you keep it a secret all this time?"

"Because I knew how my family had treated you and your mother. I figured the last thing you'd want was to meet a relative from that side of the family. I decided to let you accept me as a friend and then later I would tell you the truth that we were cousins."

"Now isn't that a touching story?" Horacio said, strolling back over to where they sat.

"Yes, it is touching," Swan said, defiantly lifting her chin. "Why are we here?"

He smiled. "You'll find out soon enough. And I hope you're not holding out any hope that your SEAL boyfriend will be coming to rescue you because he won't."

"Why do you keep saying David is a SEAL

when he's not? He was in the military once but he was never a SEAL."

"Sounds like you've been conned by him just like your cousin here was conned by me," he said as if it was something to brag about. "Your lover boy *is* a SEAL and he was sent here to get the goods on you. Whether you know it or not, you've been his assignment."

Swan shook her head. "No, that's not true. I don't believe you."

"I don't care if you believe me or not but it's true. I only found out today what he's been doing and why he was sent here by naval intelligence."

Naval intelligence? Swan glanced over at Jamila, who said, "I don't know whether what he's saying is true or not, Swan, but he told me the same thing tonight."

"Why would naval intelligence suspect me of anything? It doesn't make sense." And more than that, she refused to believe David wasn't who and what he said he was.

At that moment, they heard the sound of a boat approaching. Horacio drew his gun and pointed the flashlight toward the oncoming boat. He put his gun back in place. "Hold on to that question, sweetheart. The person who will explain everything just arrived."

Swan kept her gaze trained on the boat that pulled up beside theirs and saw two people onboard. Both of them she knew. What in the world…?

She watched in shock as Rafe and Rosie came aboard. She was so focused on staring at them that she almost missed the third person who also came on board.

She gasped in shock when the person said, "Swan, you look well."

Suddenly losing her voice, Swan couldn't do anything but sit there and stare. There had to be some mistake. A very big mistake. There was no way the person standing before her was a part of this craziness.

No way.

She finally found her voice. "Georgianna? What are you doing here? What is this about?"

Thirteen

Flipper reached the boat and attached himself to the ladder on the side. Lucky for him, no one had thought to pull it up. Taking slow, deep breaths, he pulled air into his lungs while ignoring the pain in his arms and legs. He didn't want to think about just how far he'd swum, but like he'd told his friends, he'd had to try.

He quickly eased back into the water when he heard the sound of an approaching boat and was grateful the vessel pulled up on the other side from where he was hiding. He glanced at his watch. It was synchronized with the ones worn by his teammates, and he knew they would do their best to get here soon. In the meantime, there was something he had to do.

Pulling a micro audio recorder off his belt, he moved back up the ladder to peek over the railing and into the boat.

Good. Everyone's attention was on the approaching vessel and no one saw him when he attached the audio recorder that was no bigger than a dime to the interior wall of the boat. He saw Swan and Jamila seated on a bench with their hands tied behind their backs and Horacio was standing not far away. Other than a man in the cockpit, there was no one else onboard. Flipper knew that was about to change when he heard voices.

Satisfied that the conversations would be recorded, he eased back down the ladder. When his watch began vibrating, he glanced down at the text message from Bane. On our way. Had 2 take care of a little problem 1st.

Flipper wondered what kind of problem his friends had to take care of. No matter. They were on their way and that's what counted. He listened to the conversation going on in the boat as he began pulling items from his belt. He intended to be ready to crash this little party when the time came.

He shook his head, knowing Admiral Martin would be heartbroken to discover his own daughter had sold out their country.

"I hate you," Georgianna said, glaring at Swan.

Swan was taken aback by the woman's words. "Why? What have I ever done to you? To any of you?" she asked, glancing around at the people she'd assumed were friends—Rafe, Horacio and Rosie. She hurt more at seeing Rosie than the others because she'd believed the woman had been a good friend.

"They work for me and did what they were told," Georgianna said.

"Work for you?" Swan was even more confused.

"Yes. I'm in charge of the entire operation. But I'll tell you all about that later. First, let me tell you why I despise you so much. I've waited a long time to get this out in the open. When your father died and your mother would send you to us for the summer, my parents thought you were golden. They put you on a pedestal, especially my father. Did you know he called you his little island princess?"

Yes, Swan knew but she also knew her godfather hadn't meant anything by it. It was just a nickname he'd given her when she was born. All three of her godfathers called her that sometimes. "It was just a nickname, Georgianna."

"For you, it might only have been a nickname, but for me, it was Dad shifting his attention from me to you."

"Godpop 1 loves you. He wasn't shifting his attention to me, he was just being nice."

"Too nice, and I despised you for it. He had a daughter, yet any time your mother would call, he and Mom would drop everything and take off. Just because your father saved Dad's life—that meant nothing. They were all SEALs and your dad was doing his job when he died. But it was as if Dad blamed himself and he needed to make it up by being nice to you, like you were somebody special. So, with the help of some friends, I decided to change everyone's opinion of you."

It was hard for Swan to believe what she was hearing. She'd never known that Georgianna harbored such feelings. Granted she hadn't always been overnice and had a tendency to be moody, but Swan hadn't detected animosity like this.

"What did you do?" Swan asked her.

Georgianna smiled like she was proud of what she was about to say. "I set up an espionage operation out of your shop with the help of Rafe and Horacio. Then, with Rosie's assistance, I made it appear that the secret information being sent to China was being done through your jewelry."

"What!" Swan couldn't believe it. Her head was spinning from all the shocks she'd received tonight.

"I have to admit I put together a perfect plan. This guy I was sleeping with at the time assisted me by tipping off naval intelligence with what you were supposedly doing. They did their own investigation and my team and I made sure everything pointed at you. It should have been an open and shut case and you were to be arrested and charged with espionage."

As if she was tired of standing, Georgianna moved to sit on one of the benches. She frowned over at Swan. "Everything was going according to plan until the final thread of the investigation reached Director Levart's desk."

"Godpop 3?"

"See what I mean? You have three godfathers and I don't have a one," Georgianna said in a loud voice, pointing a finger at her. "You don't deserve such love and loyalty, and I intended to tarnish their image of you."

Flipper's watch vibrated and he glanced down at the text message. Here. N place. Coop got layout of boat.

He texted them back. 1 N cockpit. 4 others. 2 hostages.

He quickly received a reply from Viper. Eliminating cockpit.

Got 4 in scope. That particular text came from Bane, a master sniper.

Flipper knew that although everyone was in place, timing was everything. Georgianna had no idea her words were being recorded so he wanted to let her talk before making his move. Then there would be no way she could deny anything.

From listening to what the woman was saying, it was obvious she had mental issues. That could be the only reason to have such a deep hatred of Swan that Georgianna would go to such extremes. Georgianna assumed she'd had the perfect plan for Swan's downfall and Flipper was glad things hadn't turned out the way Georgianna intended.

Before inching up the ladder to listen to what else she was confessing, he texted the message: Will give signal.

Swan shook her head. It was obvious Georgianna's jealousy had blinded her senses and fueled her hatred. Didn't the others see it? Why were they following her blindly? Swan glanced over at Jamila and could tell by the look in her cousin's eyes that she was wondering the same thing.

"When Director Levart saw the report, he refused to believe you could be guilty of anything, especially betraying your country."

Thank God for that, Swan thought.

"He requested a thirty-day delay before agreeing to take any actions against you. Even after we made sure the investigation clearly spelled out your role in everything. There was no reason for you not to be charged," Georgianna said.

She paused a moment before continuing. "Unknown to me and the others, Director Levart went to your other two godfathers and they put their heads together to see what they could do to prove your innocence. They decided to send one of their top SEALs to find out what he could and to prove your innocence."

Swan drew in a deep breath. *Oh no, please don't let what Horacio said tonight be true. Please don't let David turn out to be someone other than what he said he was.*

Georgianna's next words ripped into Swan's heart.

"The SEAL they sent was Lieutenant David Holloway. I guess you didn't know that all the time he spent with you was nothing more than an assignment. You meant nothing to him, Swan." Georgianna laughed as if she found the entire thing amusing while Swan's heart broke.

"Imagine how amused I was to find out just how taken you were with him, while not knowing the true purpose as to why he showed up here on the island. You were played, Swan," Georgianna was saying in between laughter. "But don't worry. I sent some other members of my group to take care of him for you. I think he's dead by now."

Suddenly a deep voice at the back of the boat said, "As you can see, I'm very much alive."

Swan gasped just as the others did. Standing with legs braced apart and wearing only a pair of swim trunks with a utility combat belt around his waist, David looked like a mad badass. It was obvious everyone was shocked to see him, especially Georgianna, who had assumed he was dead.

"Drop your gun," he ordered Horacio, who was still holding his weapon on Swan and Jamila.

"How the hell did you get here?" Horacio asked, enraged.

"I swam from Swan's home."

"That's impossible!"

"Not if you're a SEAL master swimmer," David said. "Now, do like I said and put your gun down."

"And if I don't? It will be a shame if I kill Swan or Jamila before you can get to anything on that belt you're wearing," Horacio sneered.

"Don't try it, Horacio. One of my team members who's a master sniper has all four of you within his scope. Before you could get off the first shot, you'd be dead."

"I don't believe you. There's no one else out here," Horacio said. When he lifted his gun to take aim at Swan, a shot rang out, hitting the man in the chest. The impact toppled him to the floor.

Jamila screamed and Swan understood. Jamila

had fallen in love with a man who'd betrayed her and then gotten shot right before her eyes.

Suddenly, Rafe dived for the gun that had dropped from Horacio's hand. Before he could reach it, another shot rang out that hit him in the side. He fell to the floor as well.

"Either of you ladies want to join them?" Flipper asked Georgianna and Rosie.

Rosie looked like she was in shock and ready to pass out.

However, Georgianna looked furious. "You won't get away with this. No matter what you tell my father, he will never believe you over me," she said with absolute certainty. "I'll tell him that you decided to team up with Swan and she turned you against your country."

"I figured you would lie. That's why I've recorded your little confession to Swan detailing everything. I can't wait for your father to listen to it."

Suddenly the boat was surrounded by several naval vessels and sharp beams of light shined on them. A voice through a foghorn said, "Lieutenant Holloway, we are coming aboard."

A dozen men wearing SEAL gear rushed on board with their guns drawn, immediately taking Georgianna and Rosie into custody. Bane, Viper, Coop and Mac boarded the boat as well. Mac rushed over to check Horacio and Rafe. There really was no need since they were both dead.

Flipper rushed over to Swan and Jamila to untie their hands. More than anything, he wanted to pull Swan into his arms and tell her he loved her. He wanted her to put out of her mind what Georgianna had said about him until she'd heard his side of things. However, he knew when she pulled away from him to give her cousin a hug that she didn't want to give him a chance to explain.

He didn't intend to let her walk away.

"We need to talk, Swan," he said, looking down at her.

She glared up at him. "We have nothing to say to each other. Your assignment is over, Lieutenant Holloway. Now leave me alone."

Fourteen

Two weeks later

"How long are you planning to be mad at the world, Swan?"

Swan glanced over at Candy. Her best friend had returned to the Keys after hearing about what happened and she'd decided to stay. Swan was glad Candy had returned home but she was saddened by what had brought her back.

"I am not mad at the world," Swan said, taking a sip of her orange juice.

"But you are still mad at one particular man,"

Candy said, coming to sit beside Swan on the sofa.

Swan couldn't deny that was true so she didn't. "And what if I am?"

"He had a job to do, Swan. He was given orders. Surely you understand that."

Swan glared at Candy. "I'm sure none of my godfathers' orders included sleeping with me."

"I'm sure they didn't but David didn't force himself on you."

"No, but he deceived me."

"So did the others."

Did Candy have to remind her? "And I'm not talking to them either."

That wasn't totally true since Swan had reached out to Georgianna where she was being held at a federal prison in Orlando. The woman had refused to see her. Swan knew Georgianna was undergoing psychiatric evaluations to see if she was fit to stand trial.

Swan's godparents were heartbroken and she understood how they felt. Like her, they'd had no idea Georgianna harbored such hatred toward Swan, enough to do what she'd done. With both

Rafe and Horacio dead, it was Rosie who was singing like a bird, telling everything she knew for a lessened sentence.

According to Rosie, Georgianna had manipulated a number of the men at naval intelligence into doing whatever she wanted them to do. When you were the admiral's daughter, you could wield that kind of power. She had even threatened a few with blackmail. She'd deliberately recorded several of the men having sex with her and then threatened to give the tape to her father and accuse them of rape.

Some of the men were not only married but a number were high-ranking military officers. Fearful of court-martial, the men had done whatever Georgianna asked, including falsifying records. So far, more than twelve men had been named in the scandal.

"I take it David hasn't called."

Swan drew in a deep breath. She had seen him last week when they'd had to show up at the naval station to give statements. "Yes, he's called. Several times. But I refuse to answer. Like I told him, we have nothing to say to each other. His assignment is over."

"And do you honestly think that's all you were to him, Swan?"

"Yes, but it doesn't matter."

"I think it does," Candy countered.

"And you think too much," Swan said, easing off the sofa.

The first week after the incident on the boat, she had closed her shop while naval investigators did a thorough search of Rafe's tattoo parlor. She had used that time to take care of Jamila, who was still broken up over Horacio. Jamila had loved him and in a single night had seen him become an abusive monster, a man she hadn't known. Then in the end, Jamila had watched him die before her eyes.

Swan knew Jamila was going through something that only time could heal. That's why when Swan had reopened the shop this week and Jamila had asked for extra work hours, Swan had given them to her.

"So what are you going to do?" Candy asked her.

Swan glanced over at her. "About life? Work?"

"No, about David."

Swan just couldn't understand why Candy couldn't accept that David was no longer in the equation. "I'm a survivor, Candy. Although it was hard, I made do after my parents' deaths and I will make do now." She glanced at her watch. "I'm getting dressed to go into the shop today. The cruise ship comes into port tomorrow, so business will pick up. I want to make sure most of my new pieces are on display."

Another thing they had found out was that Horacio had been fired from the cruise ship months ago but hadn't told Jamila. He had moved into Rosie's place while the woman had been gone. The duplicity of the people she'd thought she knew simply amazed Swan.

"And I need to be on my way," Candy said. "I promised my folks we would go out to dinner tonight. You can join us if you like."

"Thanks for the invite, but I'll pass. I just want to have a relaxing evening here tonight. I might go swimming on the beach later."

Swan had called Jamila and told her she would

bring lunch from their favorite sandwich café. However, there were no clients in her shop when Swan got there, so she decided to do something she usually didn't do, which was close for lunch.

Normally, the shop remained open and she and Jamila would alternate lunch duties. But today she wanted to check on Jamila, talk to her to see how she was faring. Although Swan had been there for Jamila last week, they hadn't had a real honest-to-goodness talk since Jamila had admitted to being her cousin.

"What are you doing?" Jamila asked when Swan put up the Closed sign and pulled down the blinds.

Swan smiled over at her. "New store policy. From here on out, we will close at noon for lunch."

"What about the sales you'll lose?"

Swan shrugged. "Sales aren't everything. Besides, it's just for an hour. Come join me in my office."

"All right, let me grab some sodas out of the refrigerator."

A few minutes later, she and Jamila were enjoying their lunch when Swan gave Jamila a long look. "How are you doing?"

Jamila shrugged. "Okay, I guess. Trying to move on. I loved Horacio so much only to find out he wasn't the man I thought he was."

"I know the feeling."

"No, you don't."

Swan snatched her head up, frowning. "Excuse me?"

"I said you don't know the feeling, Swan. David Holloway was nothing like Horacio. David intended to save you and Horacio would have killed me if that woman had ordered him to do so. Big difference."

"But like you, I was betrayed."

"How?" Jamila countered. "Your godfathers sent David Holloway here to prove your innocence and he did."

Jamila put her soda can down and then added, "And another thing. What man takes a chance and swims across the ocean to save a woman? Do you know how far from land we were? Think about that."

Swan had news for her—she *had* thought about it. She could never forget how David had appeared seemingly out of nowhere on that boat, looking tough and ready to kick asses while wearing nothing more than an outlandishly tight pair of swim trunks with a military belt around his waist. Even when she'd been in what seemed like a dire situation, that hadn't stopped the woman in her from noticing how dangerously sexy he'd looked at that particular moment.

"When I mentioned what an astounding feat he'd accomplished to his friends," Jamila said, reclaiming Swan's attention, "they said that's why they call him Flipper. Did you know that's his code name as a SEAL?"

Swan wiped her mouth with a napkin. "Yes, I knew he was called Flipper. But no, I didn't know it had anything to do with him being a SEAL because I didn't know he was one. I assumed Flipper was his nickname."

Swan forced from her mind the day she'd asked him about those dolphin tattoos. He'd told her then they represented Flipper. That had been the day they'd made love in this office. Right here on this desk.

She wished she wasn't thinking so hard about that now.

She looked over at Jamila. "Why are we talking about me instead of you?"

"Because I think you should and because I think I should," Jamila continued. "Talking about your situation actually helps me believe that not all men are jerks and that there are some who still possess real honor, Swan. Whether you want to admit it or not, David Holloway is an honorable man. He couldn't help being attracted to you any more than you could help being attracted to him."

Swan stuffed the wrappings from her sandwich into the empty bag. "Now you sound like Candy."

"Maybe there's a reason why I do," Jamila said, stuffing her own wrappings into a bag. "It might be because Candy and I can see things that you refuse to see. I often think about what could have happened to us had David and his friends not shown up when they did. Do you ever think of that?"

Swan drew in a deep breath. "I try not to."

"I think you should," Jamila said, standing. "Thanks for bringing lunch. It will be my treat the next time." She then walked out of the office.

Swan stayed in her office after Jamila left, trying to put their conversation out of her mind. She was working on her computer, verifying inventory, when her office phone rang. "Thank you for calling Swan's. How may I help you?"

"Hello, island princess."

She smiled upon hearing her godfather's voice. "Godpop 2. How are you?"

"I'm fine. I just wanted to check on you. So much has happened and I wanted to make sure you're okay."

She had spoken to each of her godfathers and had thanked them for believing in her. They had taken a risk with their individual careers to do that. "I'm fine. How is Godpop 3?"

"He's fine but as the director of naval intelligence, he has his hands full with the investigation. It seems that more names are popping up in this scandal each day."

"And how are Godpop 1 and Barbara?"

"They are as well as can be expected under the circumstances. Learning about Georgianna was a shocker for all of us. We had no idea. When we decided to send Lt. Holloway to prove your innocence, the three of us weren't sure just what he would uncover. The only thing we knew for certain was that you weren't guilty of anything."

"Thanks for believing in me."

"You have Andrew's blood in your veins. You could no more be a traitor to your country than he could. Considering all that happened, I'm glad Holloway remained in Key West when he could have left."

Swan sat up straight. "Wasn't David on assignment?"

"Not the entire time. His assignment officially ended when he sent that ink in to be analyzed and we discovered it was tainted. I told him that he no longer had to stay in the Keys since by then we knew you weren't involved and we would take over the investigation from there."

"Then why did he stay?"

"To protect you."

"He told you that?" she asked.

"Yes. I remember the conversation like it was yesterday. I told him he could consider his job assignment complete and go home to Texas and enjoy the remainder of his leave. But he said he wanted to hang around Key West for a while."

Her godfather paused. "I asked him if the reason he wanted to stay was because he thought your life might be in danger. He said he felt that as long as Duggers and Jacinto didn't know they were suspects, then no, your life wasn't in any immediate danger. He informed me that the reason he wanted to stay was because you had come to mean a lot to him. I told him in that case how he spent the rest of his leave was his decision. And, Swan?"

She drew in a deep breath. "Yes?"

"As his commanding officer, I felt the need to remind him that although he was no longer on assignment, since the issue that had started with you was an ongoing investigation, he could not tell you anything."

When Swan didn't reply, her godfather asked, "You're still there, Swan?"

"Yes, Godpop 2, I'm still here."

"Did you not know how Holloway felt about you?"

"No. I thought I was just an assignment."

"You were at first and I'm glad you were. Otherwise you would be in jail wrongly accused of a crime you hadn't committed. But on the flip side, I'm also glad that when you stopped being an assignment, Holloway had the insight to stay and look out for you because he cared for you."

Long after her telephone conversation with her godfather ended, Swan remained seated at her desk, leaning back in her chair and sitting in silence while thinking about what Candy, Jamila and her godfather had said.

Some people never got betrayed, but she had been, a lot. William, Rafe, Horacio, Rosie, Georgianna and even Jamila. No one had been who she'd thought.

She remembered David and replayed in her

mind all the time she'd spent with him since that day he'd first walked into her shop.

Was anything he'd told her true? Did he really come from a huge family? Was his mother even celebrating a birthday? Did he honestly have three sisters-in-law?

One thing was for certain, both Candy and Jamila were right. David hadn't pushed her into sleeping with him. In fact, Swan was the one who'd invited him to dinner at her place with the full intent of having sex with him.

She got up from her desk and walked over to the window. She knew from Jamila that David had left the island with his friends after that first week, after he'd completed all the questioning by naval intelligence. Was he back home in Texas? Did his parents really own a medical supply company? What parts of what he'd told her were true and what parts were fabricated for his assignment?

And why did she still love him so much it hurt… even when she didn't want to love him? Even when she didn't know how he felt about her? He might have told her godfather he cared for her but David hadn't told her anything. Shouldn't he have? But then, had she given him a chance to do so?

The answer to that flashed in her mind quickly. No, she hadn't.

He had saved her life that night, swam across the ocean to do so, and then she'd told him she didn't want to talk to him. And he had honored her wishes…for that one night. Then he had called her almost every single day since, and yet she had refused to take his calls.

He hadn't called today.

Did that mean he'd given up and wouldn't try contacting her again? Was she ready to put her heart on the line and contact him?

She wasn't sure. But what she *was* certain of was that they needed to do what they hadn't done before. They needed to get to know each other. She needed to know which parts of what he'd told her about himself were true and which were false.

She wanted to get to know the real David Holloway.

Then what?

Hadn't she convinced herself she wanted no part of a man in the military? And what about her decision to never to get seriously involved in an interracial relationship like her parents had? Why did all of that no longer matter to her when she thought about her and David deciding to have a future together?

Maybe that's how love worked. It made you see the possible instead of the impossible. It made you want things you told yourself were not good for you because you were afraid to reach beyond your comfort zone.

Taking a deep a cleansing breath, she decided to call David tonight before going to bed. She had no idea what she would say to him but the words would come.

She doubted he would want to come back to the Keys anytime soon, so she would let him know she would come to him if he still wanted to talk. She would see what he said before asking Jamila if she could take care of the shop while Swan was gone. David might very well tell her that it was too late, that they had nothing to talk about. But there was a chance he would embrace her words. Embrace her.

Her mood suddenly lightened, knowing that was a possibility.

Flipper entered the hotel room and tossed his luggage on the bed. Different hotel but same city. He had given Swan two weeks and now he was back. They needed to talk and clear up some things. She hadn't accepted his calls, but now he was here and he wouldn't be ignored.

He shook his head when his cell phone rang. "Yes, Coop?"

"Have you seen her yet?"

"No, I just got here. In fact, I walked into my hotel room less than five minutes ago."

"Okay. And there's another reason I called. Bristol is pregnant."

"Wow, man. Congratulations. I didn't know you guys were trying."

Coop laughed. "We're always trying. But seriously, we figured it was time Laramie had a playmate."

"Sounds good to me."

"I hope things work out with you and Swan, Flipper."

"I hope so, too."

"And do me a favor."

"What?"

"For once, open up. Tell her how you feel. Don't beat around the bush. You have a tendency to do that. Women love a man to get straight to the point and share their feelings. I hate to say it, bro, but you're not good at doing that."

Coop was right, he wasn't. "I never had to do that before. I've never truly loved a woman before Swan."

"I understand. But you do love her, so make sure she knows it. A woman has to believe she's loved."

Flipper chuckled.

"What's so funny?" Coop asked him.

"You're giving relationship advice. Do you know how much like Mac you sound?"

Coop chuckled as well. "You would have to point that out. I guess it comes with loving a woman."

"I guess so."

"No guess in it, remember it. Know it. Feel it. Take care and good luck."

After ending the call with Coop, it wasn't long before Flipper got calls from Bane, Viper and Mac as well, all letting him know they hoped things worked out for Flipper and Swan. All giving him advice. They were married men who had the women they loved and they wanted him to have the woman he loved as well.

He appreciated good friends who not only watched his back but who also cared about the condition of his heart. They knew about the pain he had lodged there and it got worse every day he and Swan were apart.

Flipper glanced at his watch. Swan's store would be closing in less than an hour. He would give her time to get home and relax before paying her a visit. He refused to let her put things off any longer. They needed to talk.

He loved her and it was damn time she knew it.

Fifteen

Swan had just poured a glass of wine to enjoy while sitting on the patio when she heard the knock at her door.

She knew Candy had gone out to dinner with her family and Jamila had mentioned she would just stay in tonight and chill. Swan had invited Jamila to join her so maybe her cousin had changed her mind.

Her cousin.

That was taking a lot of getting used to but Swan knew her parents would want a family connection for them. Jamila was the only family

Swan had and she appreciated their friendship more than ever.

She reached the door and glanced through the peephole. Her heart nearly stopped.

Was it really David? She blinked and looked again and saw it was really him. Back in Key West. And he was standing in front of her door looking like he always did, sexy as hell.

Drawing in a deep breath, she removed the security lock and opened the door. "David? I thought you'd left the island."

"I had but I returned today. May I come in?"

She nodded and stepped aside. The moment he passed her, she caught a whiff of his masculine scent, the same one she was convinced still lingered in her bedroom.

Swan closed the door and stood to face him. He was standing in the middle of her living room wearing a pair of shorts and a sleeveless shirt with a huge picture of a dolphin. *Flipper.* Her gaze moved beyond the shirt to his face to find his laser-blue eyes staring at her.

She cleared her throat. "I was about to sit out

back and drink a glass of wine while enjoying the view. Would you like to have a beer and join me?"

She could tell he was surprised by her invitation. She hadn't bothered to ask why he was there.

"Yes, I'd like that."

Moments later, they were sitting side by side on a bench that overlooked the beach. They had been sipping their drinks for a few moments when he said, "I told you that night two weeks ago that we needed to talk, Swan. I think we still do."

Yes, they did. She would let him go first. "Okay, I'm listening."

"I want you to do more than just listen, Swan. I want you to engage by asking questions, giving me feedback, and I would like to be able to do the same with you."

"Okay, that seems fair because I do have some questions for you."

"Ask away."

She took another sip of her drink. "You didn't tell me you were a SEAL and I'd—"

"I couldn't tell you I was a SEAL, Swan," he

interrupted to say. "That's why I lied and said I was no longer in the military."

"Yes, I know that now. I want to tell you, because of what happened to my father, I had made up my mind never to get serious about a military man...especially not a SEAL."

"Oh, I see."

She wouldn't tell him yet that she'd changed her mind about that. "Is your mother's birthday really next month and do you have four brothers?"

"Yes. Everything I told you about my family is true. I never lied to you about anything pertaining to them. I just omitted some details and couldn't elaborate on certain things."

She then put her wineglass down and turned toward him. "Why did you sleep with me, David, when I was just an assignment to you?"

Flipper knew this was the time of reckoning and what he told her would have an impact on their relationship for the rest of their days. He needed her to understand.

"You were supposed to be an assignment, Swan.

But honestly, I don't think you ever were. From the moment I walked into your shop and saw you, a part of me knew I had to fight hard to be objective and do the job I'd been sent here to do."

He paused. "I tried to keep my attraction to you out of the picture but found it harder and harder to do. Each time I saw you while getting to know you, I fell deeper under your spell. It was hard pretending with you."

He decided to be totally honest with her. "Just so you know, that day you invited me to your place for dinner wasn't my first time there. I'd been to your home without you knowing anything about it. But at the time, it was just a house I was checking out as part of an investigation. The day you invited me to dinner, I saw it through another pair of eyes. Yours. And for me, it then became your home."

She drew in a deep breath. "You invaded my privacy by letting yourself into my home, but that's not why I'm upset. I accept that you had a job to do and I was your assignment but…"

"But what?"

"You still haven't fully answered my question, David. Why did you make love to me?"

David frowned, realizing that he *hadn't* answered her question. His teammates often teased him about beating around the bush, sometimes providing too much context instead of just sticking with the facts.

"The reason I made love to you, Swan, was because I desired you. Everything about you turned me on. Your looks, your scent, your walk...and then after our first kiss, it was your taste. Fighting my desire for you was no longer an option, although I tried being honorable enough not to seduce you."

"But then I seduced you," she said quietly.

He smiled. "No, I think that night we seduced each other. Everything we did was mutual."

"Yes, it was." She took another sip of her wine. "I spoke with Godpop 2 today and he told me your assignment ended but you decided to stay. Why?"

Okay, no beating around the bush this time, Flipper decided. "The reason is that by then I had fallen in love with you. In all honesty, in my heart you stopped being an assignment the first time I made love to you. I crossed the line of what was honorable, and I knew why. Because I felt you here, Swan," he said, pointing to his heart. "I felt you here in a way I've never felt before. No woman has ever been here, Swan. But during the one time you shouldn't have, you got there anyway."

"And now? How do you feel now?"

He placed his beer bottle aside and turned toward her. "Now you are still in my heart. Even more so. I love you so much I ache on the inside when I'm not with you. I love you so much I think of you even at times I shouldn't."

He reached out and took her hand in his. "Now I need to know, Swan, just how you feel about me."

Swan felt the gentle tug on her hand and, surprising even herself, she moved to sit in his lap.

When he wrapped his arms around her, she felt comfort flow through her. She turned in his lap to look down at him. He'd given her answers to all her questions, now she intended to give him answers to his.

"I love you, David. I fought it at first. I didn't know about you being present-day military, but I also had a problem…not with interracial dating…but with allowing anything to come of it. I saw how others saw my parents at times. Not as a beautiful couple in love but as an interracial couple in love. There should not have been a difference. I never wanted to deal with what they had to deal with in the name of love."

She paused. "But then I moved beyond thinking that way after I fell in love with you. Then I realized how my parents must have felt, believing nothing mattered but their love. Even if the world was against them, as long as they had each other, that's what truly counted."

"So you do love me?" he asked her as if for clarity.

Swan didn't have a problem clarifying anything for him or anyone else. "Yes, I love you, David Flipper Holloway." And then she lowered her mouth to his.

Shivers of profound pleasure shot through every part of Swan's body when David slid his tongue into her mouth. Sensations bombarded her as she concentrated on his taste, his scent and the way he pulled her tongue into his mouth to mate with his. And when she felt his hands inch upward and slide beneath her top, his touch made her purr.

Both his taste and his touch were awakening parts of her, making her feel alive in a way she hadn't felt since the last time they'd been together. Here at her house. In her bed.

When his fingers touched her bare breasts, using his fingertips to draw circles around her nipples, she oozed deeper into the kiss, almost feeling like melted butter in his arms.

He slowly pulled his mouth from hers and looked at her. His blue eyes were sharp and filled with the same desire she felt. "Any reason why we can't take this inside?"

She wrapped her arms around his waist. "No, there's no reason."

"Good."

And then standing with her in his arms, he carried her into the house.

"Just so you know, David, I didn't ask you all my questions," Swan said when he placed her on the bed.

David glanced down at her. "You didn't?"

"No, but I can wait. None are more earth-shattering than this is going to be. And I need this."

He caressed the side of her face with his finger. "I need this, too. I know why I need it, tell me why you do."

She met his gaze and held it while she said, "I love the feel of you inside of me. I've never felt anything so right before. So pleasurable." She smiled. "Do you know I retired my sex toy?"

He chuckled. "That's good to know."

"Um, not too much information?"

"No. Nice to know what used to be my competition," he said as he began removing her clothes. Lucky for him, she wasn't wearing much. Just a top, shorts and a thong. Flipper had discovered outside earlier that she wasn't wearing a bra. He'd noticed more than once that she liked her breasts being free and so did he.

She reached out and tugged at his T-shirt and he assisted by removing his own shorts. Then he rejoined her on the bed. Reaching out, he lifted her by the waist.

"Wrap your legs around me, Swan. I'm about to join our bodies, to make us one."

As soon as her legs were settled around his waist, his shaft touched her core. She was wet and ready. Tilting her hips, he whispered the words, "I love you," before thrusting hard into her.

"David!"

Arching her back off the bed, she provided the prefect position for his penetration to go deeper. They were a perfect fit. They always would be. Not just in lovemaking but in everything they did from here on out. They had become a team.

He began moving, slowly at first and then harder and deeper, over and over again. The only constant sounds in the room were their breathing and flesh slapping against flesh. The air surrounding them was filled with the aroma of sex.

He felt on fire, like his entire body was burning and the flames fueled his need, his desire and his love. She was looking up at him, holding his gaze, and he hoped Swan saw the depth of love in his eyes.

He clenched his jaw when he felt it, the stirring of pleasure in his groin. The feeling was slowly spreading through his body and when Swan gripped his shoulders and dug her fingers into his skin, he continued to thrust inside of her like his life depended on it.

And when she screamed out his name, he knew the same sensations that were taking him were taking her.

He drew in a sharp breath only moments before calling out her name. Multiple sensations tore into him, causing an explosion inside of him that had him bucking his body in an all-consuming orgasm. The sensations kept coming until he let go and his release shot deep inside of her.

He knew right then that he wanted her to have his baby. If not this time, another time. One day, he intended to make it happen.

Moments later, he slumped down beside her and wrapped his arms around her as he tried to get his breathing under control. After recovering from his explosive orgasm, when he was able to talk, he said, "I feel like I've been burned to a crisp."

"Hmm, speaking of burning, do you know what I thought was hot?" she asked, drawing in deep breaths of air into her lungs.

"No, what?"

"You on that boat wearing nothing but swim trunks and that military belt around your waist. Now, that was hot."

He grinned. "You liked that, huh?"

She smirked up at him when he straddled her body again. "I liked it." Then her features became serious. "I still can't believe you swam all that way to save me."

He leaned in and brushed a kiss across her lips. "Believe it."

He then pulled back and looked down at her. His expression was serious. "I'm a damn good swimmer. I'm known to be able to hold my breath underwater for long periods of time. Longer than what most would consider normal. But I wasn't sure I was going to make it to the boat, Swan. I told my friends I had to try even if I died trying because the woman I love was on that boat. That's what kept me going. That's what fueled every stroke I made into the ocean waters. And when my body felt tired, like I couldn't possibly swim another lap, I would think of a life without you and for me that was unacceptable."

He drew in a sharp breath. For a quick minute, he relived the feel of the cold water as he swam nonstop to the boat to save her, not knowing if he would make it in time. "I had to save you."

"And then I rebuffed you. I refused to have that talk you wanted."

"I understood. I had been listening to what Georgianna Martin was saying, the picture she painted. I told myself that once I talked to you and told you the truth that you would believe me. I was just giving you time to think about everything. I figured you would realize that I did care for you."

She reached up and caressed the side of his face. "You never told me you cared."

"I did. Our last night together, when you were asleep, I told you before I left that I loved you. I had planned to tell you the next day when we were together but that's when you were taken."

"And you came back," she said.

"That was always my plan, Swan. I never intended to let you go. I love you that much. And just so you know, my entire family is rooting for me. I told them about you and they can't wait to meet you. My brothers and I are giving Mom a party for her birthday next week. Will you go to Texas with me?"

When she hesitated, he added, "What I told you about them is true. My parents accept people for who they are and not how they look. Will you trust me about that?"

She met his gaze and nodded. "Yes, I will trust you and yes, I will go."

A huge smile spread across his face. "I can't wait to introduce you to everyone. And I've got the perfect thing for you to wear." He quickly eased off the bed.

She pulled herself up. "What's going on? You plan on dressing me that night?"

He glanced over his shoulder, chuckling as he pulled a small white box out of his shorts. "Something like that."

He returned to the bed and pulled her up to stand her on her feet beside the bed. Then he got down on one knee and looked up at her. "I love you, Swan. I know we have a lot of things we still need to overcome. But I believe we will do so together. Forever. Will you marry me?"

He saw tears form in her eyes when she nodded. "Yes, I will marry you."

He slid the ring on her finger and at that moment Flipper knew he was halfway to having his world complete.

He would get the other half the day she became his wife.

Sixteen

Swan glanced down at the ring David had put on her finger last week. Seeing it gave her strength and she definitely needed strength now, she thought as she entered a huge ballroom on his arm. It was his mother's sixtieth birthday party.

They had flown into Dallas last night so this would be the first time she met his family. Nervous jitters had tried taking over her stomach but a smile from David was keeping most of them at bay. He was convinced his family would love her and he had told her over and over that she was worrying for nothing. She was the woman he wanted and his family would love his choice.

"There's Mom and Dad," he said, with his arms around her shoulders as she carried his mother's gift. The same gift he'd purchased that first day he'd come into her shop.

A man she knew had to be one of David's brothers whispered something to the older couple and they turned with huge smiles on their faces.

At that moment, Swan knew David had inherited his father's eyes and that the smiles on the couple's faces were genuine. She could actually feel their warmth. David's mom was beautiful and did not look like she was sixty or that she had five grown sons.

When they reached his parents, David made the introduction. "Mom. Dad. I want you to meet the woman who has agreed to be my wife, Swan Jamison."

"It's an honor to meet you," Swan said, extending her hand to his mother.

Instead of taking it, the older woman engulfed

Swan in a huge hug. "It's wonderful meeting you as well, Swan, and welcome to the family."

"Thank you. Here's your gift. Happy birthday."

"Thank you."

She received a hug from David's father as well. Then suddenly she was surrounded and a laughing David made introductions. All his brothers had those same blue eyes and like David, they were very handsome men. She could see why when she looked at the older Holloways; they were a beautiful couple. And Swan could tell from the way Mr. Holloway looked at his wife and the way Mrs. Holloway would look back at him that the couple was still very much in love.

A few nights ago, David had shared the fact that because his mother had been married to a Navy SEAL for over forty years and had five sons who were SEALs, she counseled a number of SEAL wives who had difficulties with the frequency and longevity of their spouses' missions. Swan had been glad to hear that since she would become a SEAL's wife soon.

Because David would be leaving in less than

four months on anther mission, they hoped to marry within a year. Surprisingly, David wanted a big wedding. She agreed as long as the wedding took place in the Keys.

The logistics of having a big wedding were enormous, given he had four brothers who were SEALs on different teams. Not to mention his closest four friends were SEALs as well. That meant Swan and David had to make sure everyone would be on leave in the States at the same time.

David also introduced Swan to her future sisters-in-law and they loved her engagement ring. The three were friendly and she liked them immediately. She was also introduced to other members of David's family—his grandparents, his niece, nephews, cousins, aunts, uncles—it was obvious the Holloway family was a huge one.

"Now I want to reintroduce you to four guys who are just as close to me as brothers. As you know, they came to the Keys to assist me in proving your innocence. And even when my assignment with you ended, they didn't leave. They stayed."

She had met his four friends that night after the incident on the boat, when they'd had to give statements. She had thanked them for their help but they hadn't been officially introduced.

"Did I tell you how beautiful you look tonight, sweetheart?"

She smiled up at him as they walked across the ballroom floor to the four men and their wives. "Yes, you told me. Thank you." She, Candy and Jamila had gone shopping in Miami. She'd known this was the perfect dress when she'd seen it on a store mannequin.

Within a few minutes, she had been introduced to Brisbane "Bane" Westmoreland and his wife, Crystal; Gavin "Viper" Blake and his very pregnant wife, Layla; Laramie "Coop" Cooper and his wife, Bristol; and Thurston "Mac" McRoy and his wife, Teri.

After spending time with the couples, Swan felt that just like her future sisters-in-law, the four women were genuinely friendly and Swan looked forward to getting to know them better. They loved her engagement ring as well and told David he'd done a great job in picking it out.

"So what do you think?" David leaned down to ask, taking her hand in his and leading her to where his parents, siblings and their spouses were getting ready to take a group picture.

She grinned up at him. "Um, for starters, I think I need to start calling you Flipper, since everyone else does. And then, *Flipper*, I think I am one of the luckiest women in the world right now. I love you."

He chuckled as he pulled her to the side of the room and wrapped his arms around her waist. "And I, Swan Jamison, think I'm the luckiest man in the world, and I love you."

"A very wise woman, my mother, once told me that when you meet a man who puts that sparkle in your eyes then you'd know he was a keeper. You, Flipper, are a keeper."

He smiled. "You, my beautiful Swan, are a keeper as well."

Flipper then lowered his mouth to hers.

Epilogue

A year later in June

Bane Westmoreland leaned close and whispered to Flipper, "Don't get nervous now. You wanted a big wedding and you got it."

Flipper couldn't say anything because Bane was right. He stood flanked by his father, who was his best man, and twelve groomsmen—namely his brothers, best friends and cousins.

Only his SEAL teammates knew Flipper had a tendency to tap his finger against his thigh when he was nervous. He stopped tapping but not because he noticed that Viper, Mac and Coop were grinning over at him. But then he figured both Viper and Coop had reasons to grin since they'd both become fathers this year. Viper was the proud father of a son, Gavin IV, and Coop had a beautiful daughter they'd named Paris, since that was where he'd first met his wife.

It was a beautiful day for a beach wedding and so far everything was perfect and going according to plan. Swan had hired one of the local wedding planners and the woman had done an awesome job. She had thought of everything, including the super yacht that could hold their five hundred guests that they'd be using for the wedding reception. It was anchored in the ocean near Swan's beachfront home. A fleet of passenger boats had been chartered to transport the wedding guests out to the yacht.

A ten-piece orchestra sat beneath towering balustrades draped from top to bottom in thin white netting. Chairs were set up on the beach, auditorium style, facing the decorative stage where

Flipper and the men in the wedding party stood waiting.

Suddenly, the music began and all the ladies strolled down the beach and up the steps.

Swan had chosen her wedding colors of purple and yellow and Flipper had to admit the combination was striking. It took all twelve women long enough to do their stroll. His niece was a flower girl and Coop's son and one of Flipper's nephews were the ring bearers.

Flipper almost held his breath when what looked like a huge forty-foot golden swan was rolled onto the beach. When the orchestra changed their tune for the "Wedding March," the swan opened and his Swan appeared in a beautiful, dazzling white gown. She looked beautiful, stunning and breathtaking all rolled into one.

Flipper stared at the woman who would be his wife and felt so much love in his heart. He hadn't known until now just how much he could feel for one woman. They had spent the past year deepening their friendship and their love. He looked forward to returning from his covert operations, knowing she would be there waiting on him.

He watched as she slowly strolled toward him. All three of her godfathers participated in walking her up the aisle, passing her off to the other so many feet along the way. Then all three of them gave her away. When Swan reached his side and extended her hand to him, he accepted it while thinking she was *his* Swan.

His beautiful Swan.

The wedding ceremony began. What Flipper would remember most when he looked back was when the minister announced them husband and wife and told him he could kiss his bride.

Flipper pulled Swan into his arms and lowered his mouth to hers. She was his and he intended to keep her happy for the rest of his days. They would be flying to Dubai for a two-week honeymoon and then return to the Keys where they planned to make their permanent home.

When David released Swan's mouth, the minister said, "I present to everyone David and Swan Holloway."

Flipper knew they were supposed to exit by walking down the golden steps that led to the boat that would transport them to the yacht. But at that moment, he couldn't deny himself another kiss and lowered his mouth to his wife's again.

* * * * *